It's More Than A Game!

By

Bill Collar

It's More Than A Game!
by Bill Collar
© 2007

Copyright registered with the Library of Congress

ISBN 978-1-933556-81-9

Bill Collar
421 Keune St.
Seymour, WI 54165
www.billcollar.com
pma@billcollar.com

All rights reserved. The reproduction of any part of the book for commercial use is prohibited.

Printed and bound by Publishers' Graphics, LLC

J COLLAR

About the Author

Coach Collar taught high school and coached football and track for 35 years. While at Seymour High School he was recognized as WI State Teacher of the Year, WI Football Coach of the Year, and coached state champions in football and track. He and his wife Holly raised three daughters and have seven grandchildren.

About the Illustrator

Sarah VerVoort, Coach Collar's daughter, is a elementary teacher in Shiocton, WI. As a high school student, she competed in volleyball and track, and was a national powerlifting champion. She and her husband Glen have three children.

Dedicated to

Cheyenne, Cole, Justin, Devin, James, Levi, and Hannah. Doing your best is more important than being the best!

With appreciation

A special thank you to all the players, teachers, and coaches who provided the ideas and stories on which this book is based. A tip of the coaching cap to fifth grade teacher Sandy Ladenburger for her many suggestions and discerning eye.

Cover Picture: Casey Jefson, Seymour Middle School student and athlete.

GERMANTOWN COMMUNITY LIBRARY
GE

Contents

Chapter 1

Focus On Success

It was a clear, crisp night and Jason was tossing and turning, trying to get to sleep. He looked out the window and the full moon among the twinkling stars reminded him of a big cheese pizza suspended somewhere in space.

Tomorrow was the first day of tackle football practice and Jason was worried about how he would do compared to his friends. He enjoyed playing flag football, but now he was in the seventh grade and eligible to play in the tackle program. In fact, he didn't know if he really wanted to play tackle football because it looked like a rough game. He liked to watch the Packers on television and go to the high school games, but now it was time for him to be a player. Last year his friend Kyle's older brother broke his ankle and had to be in a cast for five weeks. That didn't seem like much fun!

Jason Vershaw lived in a small community in Northeastern Wisconsin with his parents, an older sister Cheyenne, and a younger brother

Tyler. Some of the bigger cities in the area started tackle football in the fourth grade. But in his town, Scenic Valley, boys who wanted to play were limited to flag ball until they were in the seventh grade.

Even though Jason liked flag ball, he usually managed to get out of the way in the tackle games the kids would organize on weekends. He just didn't like the possibility of getting hurt. Of course those games were played without equipment; maybe he would be more aggressive when he wore a helmet and full pads.

Jason's father played football in high school. From the time he was little his dad reminded him how much he was looking forward to watching him play. Jason didn't want to let his father down. He recalled the day when they were playing catch in the yard and he told his dad that he wasn't sure he wanted to play tackle football. He said he was nervous about tackling people and having other players tackle him.

His father assured him that the coaches would teach him how to tackle and play the game with confidence. Then his dad told him something that he had been thinking about as he was tossing and turning in his upstairs bedroom. His dad's words kept going through his head,

"It's OK to be nervous, what is really important is what you do with the nervousness."

His dad explained that being worried is like being afraid, perhaps afraid of making a mistake or fear of not living up to expectations. Then he said, "Even pro athletes are nervous, but once the game starts they concentrate on doing things right and not on what might go wrong."

Pulling the covers up over his eyes to hide from the moonbeam coming through the window, Jason said to himself, *"I've got to keep thinking about what will go right!"* He dozed off wondering about how he would do at tomorrow's practice and whether or not he would like the coach.

"Cock-A-Doodle Doo" the rooster crowed as the sun glared through the pine trees. No matter how tired he was, or what day of the week it was, the rooster was a reliable alarm clock. Jason thought it was silly, but his mother, a farm girl at heart, insisted on keeping hens for eggs, and the rooster reminded her of childhood days visiting Grandpa and Grandma's farm.

Jason bounded down the steps and was greeted by the smell of pancakes frying on the stove. It was always a special treat to have applesauce and maple syrup with the pancakes. Jason's mother insisted that he eat a nutritious breakfast and reminded him, ***"In order to do your best you must eat your best."*** His mother was an elementary school teacher and had plenty to do in the morning, but she always found the time to make sure Jason, his brother, and sister had the opportunity to eat a good breakfast.

Because Jason's mother knew it was a big day for him, she was preparing his favorite breakfast. Often he would have cold cereal and fruit, but his mother never allowed him to have sugarcoated cereal. She said it was just "fluff" and he needed a nutritious meal.

As he checked his backpack, Jason made sure he had his school papers, physical card, and his new football shoes. He had been mowing lawns and doing gardening work all summer so he could save money to buy his first pair of football shoes. His mother and dad went shopping with him and made sure he purchased a durable pair that would last the entire season.

He came up a little short in paying for the shoes, but his parents pitched in the remainder. His father encouraged him to break them in by wearing them several times prior to the first practice. A blister caused by new shoes was miserable and would slow a person down. Jason felt really fast in the shoes and could cut and change direction like never before.

The big yellow bus pulled up in front of his house and Jason and his brother and sister jumped on. Behind the wheel was Mr. Ponshak. He had been driving bus for many years and always greeted the students with a "Good morning" and a friendly smile.

Jason's brother and sister in unison replied, "Good morning, Mr. Ponshak."

The driver responded, "Mr. Ponshak is my father, call me Max."

All the students respected Max and appreciated his cheery greeting to start the day.

Jason took a seat next to his classmate Rocky Swenson. His real name was Mason, but everyone called him Rocky because he was considered to be the toughest kid in the seventh grade. Last year during a basketball game, he stepped in front of a player going in for a lay-up and the opposing player just bounced right off of him.

Coach Larson had said, "You really rocked that player, I'll bet he won't drive to the basket anymore." From then on he was called Rocky.

Rocky asked, "Aren't you excited? Today is the first day of football practice. I'm looking forward to crunching someone."

Jason hoped that he wasn't the one to be "crunched."

He turned to Justin Keller, a good friend, and asked, "Did you get that writing assignment finished for language arts that is due today?" He wanted to talk about anything but football.

It was difficult to pay attention in class. No matter how much he tried to focus on his schoolwork, Jason's mind kept drifting toward football practice. What will we do the first day? Will it be tough? Will I like the coach? How will it feel to tackle someone?

Playing tackle football with pads was like getting ready to ride a two-wheel bike for the first time. The training wheels were off and now it was up to him to keep peddling. His mind flashed back to when his mom and dad encouraged him to ride the two-wheeler on his own. His mom told him that sometimes life is like riding a bike for the first time. When you fall, you just have to get right back up and keep peddling. She called it *"Persistence – keep at it until you are successful."* She reminded him,

"Success is just a matter of overcoming failure. Do your best, and you will have fun playing football with your friends."

In spite of Jason's pledge to himself to keep a positive attitude, he couldn't prevent his mind from drifting back to Rocky's comment about "crunching someone."

Reflecting on his mother's words, Jason thought, "It is easy to talk about success, but for some reason I keep thinking about failure."

Chapter 2

The Big Decision

All day Jason's mind kept going back to his parents' comments. What would they say if he came home right after school? They wouldn't be home yet. Maybe he could make up some story about practice being cancelled.

Toward the end of class, when he was convincing himself to come up with a good excuse, an announcement reminded him, "All seventh grade boys interested in playing football should report to the gym immediately after school."

"Oh gosh," Jason thought, "I'm not going to football. I'll take the bus home and say I forgot about practice."

Then he remembered the *"mirror test."* Mrs. Gruber, his sixth grade teacher, often told her students to occasionally look into the mirror and ask yourself, "Am I happy with the decisions I am making?"

He knew he wouldn't be able to pass the "mirror test" if he just ignored practice and took the bus home. He considered the situation and realized that he had to, ***"Do the right thing, because it is the right thing to do."***

Once again, he could hear Mrs. Gruber as she reminded the class that to make the correct decision you must first, ***"Gather all the information, consider the consequences, evaluate the facts, and then accept personal responsibility."***

The lesson stuck with Jason. Mrs. Gruber told the students, "Just remember the word ice." Then she wrote on the whiteboard:

I = *Information – gather all the facts.*
C = *Consequences – what could happen?*
E = *Evaluate – ask do I want to do this?*

She said, "You must realize that making decisions is an extremely important part of life. This is called accepting personal responsibility for your actions. You don't make excuses; you take action and do the right thing."

Just then he bumped into Justin Keller in the hallway. He told Jason he got a new video game for his birthday and Jason was invited over to his house to try it out.

As he was going out the back door of school with Justin, Jason saw his reflection in the glass door. It was like looking into a mirror. Suddenly he stopped, turned to his friend and said, "I almost forgot, I've got to go to a football meeting after school."

Once again, Mrs. Gruber's words came back to him. *"Do the right thing because it's the right thing to do."* He knew it was the right thing to do. He made the correct decision.

Chapter 3

Practice With A Purpose

Jason joined several of his classmates and they confidently walked to the gym. "It is amazing how a person's attitude can change when you are with your friends," Jason thought. Jason and his buddies were surprised to see the large number of seventh grade boys who were planning to play football.

Of course, Rocky Swenson was there, but he didn't realize Stretch Adams, Tank Tankson, and Bobby Benson were going to play. Stretch was the tallest boy in the class and a very good basketball player. Tank was huge, and Bobby was the fastest. Jason remembered that no one had beaten Bobby in a race since the third grade when Hannah Murphy smoked him. He said she started early. "Gosh," he thought, "it looks like the team will have plenty of athletic ability and

I'm not one of them. I'm really bad compared to many of the other players."

Jason discovered he was doing just what his mother said he shouldn't do. He was comparing himself to other students. Her words came back to him, ***"It's not what others do, what is most important is what you do. Doing your best is more important than being the best. Only one person can be the best, but everyone can do their best."***

The bleachers were pulled out on one side of the gym. Jason and two friends, Cole Christian and Levi Carter, took a seat along with over 40 other students. Just then Mr. Stackhouse, the coach and gym teacher, appeared. He was a big, tall man with legs like tree trunks and arms like telephone poles. His shaved head glistened like the hood of a brand new car.

In a deep, gruff voice Coach Stackhouse said, "I need everyone's attention." Suddenly it was as quiet as a church at midnight. The coach said, ***"I want all of you to listen with your eyes."***

Jason thought, "What?"

Coach Stackhouse explained, "When I look at you I want to see you looking back at me. That way I know you are paying attention."

Coach Stackhouse was a former star athlete at nearby Maple Grove High School. He played college ball and even had a tryout with the Detroit Lions as an offensive lineman. Jason's dad told him he was fortunate to have him as a coach. He recalled how his dad said, ***"Always listen to the coach and do what he tells you to do.*** When the coach tells you to line up for drills or to run to another part of the field, always run your fastest. The coach will know you are eager and running will help you to get in shape. ***Always practice and play with enthusiasm."***

Coach told the eager team members that the first three days of practice would consist of conditioning drills and skills tests. He mentioned that the coaches wanted to help get the players in shape and find the best position for each individual.

"Whew!" Jason thought, "what a relief. At least for a couple days I don't have to worry about lining up across from Rocky Swenson or having Tank fall on me."

Coach Stackhouse then introduced the team to his assistant, Coach Armstrong. Armstrong was a much smaller man with a lean build and a nose that looked like it had been broken a few times. He was a popular eighth grade science teacher and also coached wrestling. He was old enough to be Coach Stackhouse's father, but he looked strong for his age.

Coach Armstrong talked about making a **commitment** to attend all the practices. He emphasized how important it was to keep improving and stressed practicing to get better. He said he had been coaching for over 25 years and the thing that bothered him the most was when players just practiced to get it over. Coach talked about being better at the end of practice than at the start. Then very enthusiastically he said, *"Good, better, best, never let it rest, until your good gets better and your better gets best!"* He asked everyone to say it with him, *"Good, better, best, never let it rest, until your good gets better and your better gets best!"*

Some students didn't participate and Coach Armstrong reminded the players, *"When a team works together, everyone does their best."* The second time he had all the players stand up and emphasized that he wanted to hear everyone. The players almost blew the roof off the gym as they all chanted the slogan with the coach.

Coach Armstrong told the players that he expected that type of effort in practice and in the games. *He stressed that if you want to play your best you must practice with a purpose and the purpose of practice is to get better.* He then turned the meeting back to Coach Stackhouse who explained what was expected of each player.

Stackhouse told the team that he expected all players to do their best in school just like they are expected to do their best in football. He looked right at Stretch Adams and said, "I want everyone to leave practice a better player than when they came to practice." Then he moved over to where Bobby Benson was sitting and asked, *"Does that make sense to you Benson?"*

Bobby was startled by Coach Armstrong's enthusiasm and simply replied, "Yes sir!"

"Wow," Jason thought, "He just told the entire team that he expected a great effort from everyone. And he did it by getting in the face of the two best athletes in the seventh grade. If he is willing to get after them, and they are the best players, I better really hustle and work hard."

Jason thought, *"I'm going to practice hard and get better every day."*

Just then, his thoughts were interrupted by Coach Stackhouse's voice. "Get your gym clothes on and we will all meet on the practice field behind school."

Chapter 4

Do The Little Things Right

The locker room was so small it seemed like every time a player turned around he bumped into someone else. The seventh grade had to divide up the locker room with the eighth grade. Fortunately, the coaches staggered the dressing times, but many players had to share lockers with teammates. The conditions would be much worse after equipment was issued.

Jason hurried to get changed into his gym clothes, locked his locker, and carried his football cleats outside where benches were set up for the players to put on their shoes. Jason saw the only open spot was next to Rocky Swenson. When he sat down Rocky slid over and pushed him off the bench. "Oops, sorry!" he said sarcastically.

Several players laughed, but Jason felt better when Bobby Benson reached down to give him a hand back up. Rocky stormed away followed by his sidekick, Tank Tankson.

The practice field was located just behind school. When Jason arrived, Coach Armstrong was busy getting the players lined up for stretching. After jogging around the far goal post, the players were told to line up in eight rows with five in a row. Coach insisted that they line up in straight rows, arms width apart. He said, *"When we do the little things right, the big things happen. Today we are going to work on the little things."*

Coach Stackhouse was the last one out of the locker room. He hustled to the field and took a place up front next to Armstrong. The coaches led the players in a number of stretching exercises. Those were followed by several form running drills.

"Knees up, elbows in, pump the arms, roll from the shoulders, thumbs up, eyes level." Coach Stackhouse shouted encouragement as he demonstrated proper running form.

"Too often we waste energy and tire easily when we don't run efficiently," Coach Armstrong said.

Bobby Benson and Devin Komp were selected to come to the front and demonstrate

GERMANTOWN COMMUNITY LIBRARY
GERMANTOWN WI 53022

proper running technique.   Devin was an outstanding soccer player and many students were surprised to see him out for football. He ran with ease and seemed to bound along with smooth strides like a cheetah after prey. What a contrast to Tank who swung his arms from side to side and looked like a penguin as he bobbed his head forward and back.

After the running drills the players who wanted to be backs or receivers were directed to go with Coach Armstrong, and the linemen were to join Coach Stackhouse. Three quarters of the players reported to Armstrong. Seeing that he was short on linemen, Coach Stackhouse blew his whistle and told all the players to "take a knee" in front of him. He asked the players, "How do you

spell team?"

Brent Brixton, the class brain, shouted out, **"T-E-A-M."** Of course, everyone else knew, but he was the only one to speak up.

Coach said, ***"That's right T-E-A-M! You notice there is no I in team.*** In football you always do what is best for the **Team**." He then picked up a football and asked, "How much does the ball weigh?"

No one knew, not even Brixton. Coach answered his own question, "About 12 ounces." He flipped the ball to Rocky and said, "You see, it isn't heavy, anybody can carry it. We need linemen. It's the guys up front who open the holes for the backs. Without a tough line we won't have much of a team."

Coach Stackhouse told the team they would have a word of the day for each practice. He turned to Brixton and asked, "Brent, what do you think the word of the day is for today?"

Once again, Brains shouted, **"Team!"**

Coach Stackhouse explained, "You can go to whatever group you want right now, but understand within a couple days we will be learning plays and everyone will be assigned a position based on how you did in the drills. Go where you think you will be the greatest help to the team. What's the word of the day?"

Everyone exclaimed, ***"TEAM!"***

Thinking he had pretty good speed, Jason decided he would stay with the backs. Coach Armstrong had all the backs run through some ropes that formed a pattern on the ground, and then had them weave in and out between dummies. He concluded the drill period by dividing the players up in pairs and giving each a ball. He watched as they played catch at a distance of about ten yards apart. He said he was looking for players who could pass and catch. Jason was proud that he caught every pass that was thrown to him.

Coach emphasized, "Catch the ball with your hands and then tuck it away. When you are facing the quarterback, keep your little fingers together when catching the ball below the waist, thumbs together above the waist. When passing, keep the nose of the ball up. Follow through with your thumb down and palm out. Get the ball up by your ear as you throw. Step toward your target."

He demonstrated that throwing a football was similar to throwing a baseball, except when finishing the throw the thumb must come down instead of up.

After about 20 minutes, Coach Stackhouse blew his whistle and yelled, "Rotate." All the players who thought they were backs then had to do the line drills and all the linemen became backs. Jason now was a lineman and he learned the proper way to block and the footwork necessary to play up front.

Jason's favorite part was when Coach Stackhouse demonstrated the value of quickness. He explained that the quarterback's cadence would be, "Set, Hit, Go, and Fire." Most of the time the ball would be snapped on, "Hit!" At times, the offense would change the count to keep the defense off balance.

He stressed that the offense had an advantage because the players all knew the count. The defense would have to react to the ball or the first movement of the offense.

To demonstrate the advantage of knowing the snap count, Coach Stackhouse selected Jason to step forward. The rest of the players watched. Coach had Jason fold his hands in front of him and told him, "I am going to put my hands down by my side. You watch my hands and as soon as they move, slide your hands up or down so I can't hit them."

Jason concentrated on Coach's hands and was determined to move his hands out of the way. Coach yelled, "Set" and Jason moved his hands, but Coach held his hands motionless at his side. He said, "You just jumped offside. That is a five-yard penalty." He yelled, "Set" again, but Jason concentrated and didn't move his hands. Coach slapped both his hands over Jason's and said, "Gotcha."

Coach Stackhouse continued to show how the offense had an advantage, catching Jason every time. He emphasized, ***"Football is a game of concentration and discipline.*** We will change our snap count to keep the defense from getting the jump on us. We have to be disciplined enough to go on the correct count."

"Wow!" Jason thought, "in the past we would always snap the ball on 'Hike,' this is going to be much harder." Then he remembered what his dad often told him, ***"Anyone can do the easy things, it's how you approach the hard things that will determine whether you will be successful."*** He knew if he was going to be a good football player he had to do the hard things right.

Chapter 5

All The Way With PMA!

To finish practice Coach Stackhouse blew his whistle and called the players to him. Several of the boys in Coach Armstrong's group just walked to join the players gathered around Stackhouse. Coach looked up and with a determined expression said, ***"When you are on the football field you always run from one place to another.*** As a reminder, when I blow my whistle, I want everyone to sprint around the far goalpost and come back to this spot."

On the whistle everyone took off on a sprint. Even though he was tired, Jason was among the first six or seven to get back to Coach. In fact, everyone ran all the way. After almost all the players were finished, Tank was still plodding along about thirty yards behind. He was running hard, but was struggling with all the extra weight he had to carry. Just when it looked like he was about to stop, Coach Armstrong yelled, "Let's give him some help." He started shouting, "Go Tank, go! Go Tank, go!" Soon the entire team started yelling encouragement. Tank's face lit up and his arms started pumping. He picked up speed and finished in a sprint.

Tank came barreling into the group, but instead of stopping at Coach, he ran another five yards and sprawled out on the ground like a beached whale. As the players gathered around, Coach Stackhouse said, "Good effort Tank."

Slowly Tank got to his feet even though it seemed like his tongue was still on the ground.

Coach asked, "Are you tired?"

Tank replied, "I didn't think I'd make it."

Coach Stackhouse felt he could teach the team a good lesson and asked Tank, "It looked like you were going to stop, and then all of a sudden you started sprinting. What happened?"

Tank replied, "I heard the guys yelling. They gave me confidence."

Coach turned to the team and said, "That's what teamwork is all about. Remember this, sometimes you may doubt yourself or think that you can't do it, but the team is counting on you."

Coach Stackhouse asked, "What is the word of the day?

"Team!" the players replied.

"That's **T-E-A-M, Together Everyone Achieves More,"** Coach reminded them.

Then he said something that Jason had heard before, **"Always keep a positive mental attitude. You control the way you feel about things. Most of all, believe in yourself and go All the way with PMA!"** Always believe in yourself!

His fifth grade gym teacher, Mr. Larson, encouraged students to do the same thing. He called that type of thinking, "Having a positive attitude." He recalled how Mr. Larson would say, "Today let's go *All the way with PMA!*"

He never really understood what that meant until one day when Mr. Larson was teaching the class how to jump rope, a student was having trouble, threw down the rope, and said, "I can't do it!"

Mr. Larson asked, "Where is your *PMA*?"

"My what?"

"Your PMA, your *Positive Mental Attitude*." He went on to tell the entire class that he never wanted to hear anyone say, "Can't."

He stated that it was all right to say, "I'm having difficulty, but never can't. Can't is short for cannot, which means never. But having difficulty means with practice, patience, and belief, eventually success will follow."

Jason remembered how Mrs. Gruber, when teaching social studies, talked about Martin Luther King, Jr., the great civil rights leader, and how he emphasized that it was important to, *"Keep your eyes on the prize."* It was then that Jason realized he could only reach the prize if he believed in his ability to accomplish the task. He was determined to go, *"All the way with PMA!"*

Chapter 6

Pound Ground to Gain Ground

The story was, that while wrestling in high school at the state tournament, Coach Armstrong was taken down off the mat and broke his nose on the floor. His coach stopped his nose from bleeding, stuffed it with cotton, and he went back and pinned his opponent to win the state championship.

With his reputation as a state champion wrestler and former varsity wrestling coach, Coach Armstong was highly respected by the students and their parents. He also was an outstanding science teacher who had a knack for keeping the class interesting.

He taught at the eighth grade level, but to help his friend Coach Stackhouse, Armstrong coached seventh graders. Jason looked forward to having him as a teacher in another year. Mr.

Armstrong was noted for his creative approach to teaching science. One of his most popular experiments was to have students pack a raw egg in a box and drop it from the second floor science room window onto the sidewalk. Students used a variety of packing materials, but very few eggs survived the fall.

His approach to coaching was similar. For example, he used the wall of a storage shed to teach the proper position to be in when blocking. Coach Armstrong believed one of the most difficult things in football was to be an effective blocker.

It was the second day of football and Jason was a little stiff as he jogged out to the practice field. The coaches told the players they would be sore from the different exercises and drills that they did yesterday. As Jason progressed through the stretching and running drills, he felt his muscles loosen up just as the coaches said they would.

He also noticed that a few players were missing from practice. After stretching, Coach Stackhouse brought the team together and asked about the four players who were missing. "Does anyone know where Bobby Markins is? What about Dustin Schultz? Did anyone see Dennis Mulroy? How about Josh Young?"

Bobby was absent from school, but Dustin, Dennis, and Josh just didn't show up for practice.

Devin Komp, a friend of Dustin's, said he went home because he was too sore. Bobby Bensen said that Dennis told him that practice wasn't any fun and he quit. Nobody knew anything about Josh.

Jason could see that Coach Stackhouse was upset. Coach reminded the players that he had told them if they find that football is not for them, the proper thing to do is to talk it over with their parents and then speak with one of the coaches. He related that football wasn't for everyone, but *it was everyone's responsibility to talk with the coaches if they decide they don't want to play. He said when people act responsibly they think of others and not just themselves.*

Coach said he would speak with Dustin and Josh, but in the future, anyone who just decided to miss practice without an excuse would be dropped from the team. He emphasized that the team was counting on each individual and *every player had a responsibility to the team to be at practice and do his best while at practice.*

In fact, Coach Stackhouse said, "*Responsibility* is the word of the day!"

"What is the word-of-the-day?" Coach asked.

The team shouted, "*Responsibility!*"

"It is your responsibility to do your best, to be at practice, and to play your hardest. You also have a responsibility to your parents to be at practice and to improve. The team is counting on you, the coaches are counting on you, and your parents are counting on you." Coach Stackhouse raised his voice and said, "Every player must make a *commitment* to the team!"

The coaches divided the team into two groups: offensive linemen, and backs and receivers. The procedure was similar to the first practice when the players chose which group to join.

Jason went with the backs and receivers with a couple of his friends, Cole Christian and Levi Carter. Cole was tall and lean and caught the ball really well. He wanted to be a wide receiver. Levi was shorter, with a stocky build. He wanted to be a running back. Both of them had good speed, but Jason knew he could beat them in a short sprint.

Jason really didn't know where he wanted to play, but felt being a back or receiver would be more fun than playing in the line. His group started off by learning how to take handoffs and running over dummies. Next they worked on protecting the ball and how to drop the shoulder to deliver a blow when getting tackled. Coach even showed them how to get their head up when going down. Keeping the head up helped bring the feet back under the runner to regain balance. His group finished with several pass-receiving drills.

Jason thought he did all right, but noticed that he didn't catch the ball as well as Cole. And Levi sure looked good doing the hit and spin drill when running with the ball.

After what seemed like a half hour Coach Stackhouse blew his whistle, made a few comments, and sent the group over to Coach Armstrong. Jason thought it was neat how the coaches would bring the players together at the end of the drills and review the major things they accomplished. He also liked the idea that the coaches kept them moving and there was little standing around.

While sprinting to Coach Armstrong's area Jason led the pack. As he turned to see that he was ahead, Bobby Benson passed him. Jason gave it his all and both of them impressed the coach.

Coach Armstrong told them, ***"Good hustle,*** Vershaw and Benson."

Jason thought, ***"Just like my dad told me, when you hustle you get noticed."***

The players were directed to line up next to the wall of the storage shed. He explained that everyone has to know how to block, and in this session he would teach the proper way to do it. Coach moved over to the wall and told the players that the wall represented the defensive man. He moved back from the wall, arched his back and squatted until his fingertips touched the grass. Coach Armstrong  put his hands on the wall next to his eyes and said, "This is what the perfect blocking position should look like."

He selected Levi and asked him to step forward. Coach told the rest of the players to watch closely as he directed Levi to stand straight, arms length from the wall with his feet at armpit width. He directed Levi to squat down and touch his fingertips to the ground while keeping his chest up. Then he had him put his hands on the wall next to his eyes that happened to be about the height of a line on the wall.

Coach told him to rock forward until both heels were off the ground. He pointed out to the rest of the players, "Notice Levi has his head up, back arched, shoulders a little higher than his hips, feet armpit width apart, with his toes pointing straight ahead. This is the position we want you to be in when blocking."

He emphasized keeping the head up because that was the strongest and safest position. Coach then had all the players move forward and go through the same procedure while their partner stood behind them and made sure they were in the proper blocking position.

Coach Armstrong stressed that it is important to move the defender off the line of scrimmage. In order to do that, good leg drive is required. The next step was to pump the legs while maintaining the correct blocking position against the wall. He referred to this as, "foot fire." It was like running with short, choppy steps. Coach encouraged the players to, "*Pound ground to gain ground.*"

He stressed that the key to blocking and tackling was to have live, active feet. Time and time again coach emphasized bending the knees and driving the legs.

Just as the players were starting to catch on, the whistle blew and Coach Stackhouse gathered the team for a few final words.

"What is the word of the day?" he asked.

Almost all of the players shouted, "*Responsibility!*"

Coach reviewed that each player had a responsibility to his teammates, coaches, parents and himself. He concluded practice by reminding everyone that they also had a responsibility to do their best in school. He expected everyone to be a "winner" on and off the field.

Chapter 7

I Think I Can

Jason woke up looking forward to school. Always a pretty good student, he liked to read, but was a bit nervous about reading aloud in class. It was especially challenging because several of his friends were better readers than he was and he kept comparing himself to them. He knew he shouldn't be doing that, but it was difficult not to. Fortunately, his teachers were patient and understanding. They made Jason feel like he was getting better all the time.

Jason had five classes with four women teachers and a man. He was pleased to have a male teacher. Other than Mr. Larson, the gym teacher, his only other male teacher had been Mr. Benkowski in the third grade. Jason really liked how Mr. B. taught social studies and often had students working on exciting history projects.

Jason vividly remembered how Mr. B. had his students take the identity of a famous person from history for a day. The students were required to dress like that person, participate in a class discussion, and bring in something the person may have used. Students could also make drawings, write a poem, or sing a song about the famous person.

Mr. B. provided the students with a list of about forty famous people from which to choose. After considerable thought, Jason selected Davey Crockett, the hero of the Alamo. He recalled with pride how he stood in front of the class in his coonskin cap and sang the song summing up Crockett's life. The entire class joined in the chorus, "Da-vey, Da-vey, Crockett, king of the wild frontier."

He also participated in the class spelling bee, won several math contests, and had a major role in the winter holiday program.

Now he was in the seventh grade where there seemed to be more teasing and gossiping. The eighth graders knew their way around, and some of them intentionally gave the wrong directions if the seventh graders asked how to get to a classroom.

Fortunately, the teachers were in the hallway between classes. They were friendly and that helped make the changes easier to accept. He especially liked two teachers.

Mrs. Kohler, his Spanish teacher, was very enthusiastic. He knew nothing about Spanish, but it sounded exciting when she talked about all the projects they would be doing. He was looking forward to building his "Family Tree." Jason knew little about his ancestors and thought it would really be neat to do even though he would have to use Spanish words to describe them.

Mr. Palbitski, the gym teacher, told the students to call him Mr. P. Some students thought his name was kind of funny, but they were all impressed the first day of class when he climbed a rope to the top of the gym without using his legs. Mr. P. promised many games and a lot of fun, but Jason was looking forward to the strength-training unit. He knew it would help him get stronger for sports.

Mr. P. encouraged the students to do push-ups and sit-ups to help build up basic strength prior to beginning the strength-training unit. One day in class he did ten push-ups using only one arm. He told Jason he would teach him how to do some when Jason could do 20 flat-back push-ups with both arms.

Sitting in seventh hour language arts class, Jason thought the big hand of the clock would never get to the top. He was eager to get to football practice. Today was the third day and Coach said practice would be a little shorter so the players could pick up their equipment. He was looking forward to getting his shoulder pads and helmet.

Practice started with a review of the word-of-the-day for the past two practices. At Coach's prompting the players yelled out, *"TEAM"* and then *"Responsibility."*

"You've got it," Coach Stackhouse replied. "The word for today is *Attitude."* He went on to say, "It is the way you approach each practice. When you have a positive attitude you expect to be successful, you believe in yourself, your coaches, and your team. I like to call it a *"Positive Mental Attitude."* He asked the players how many had read the book *THE LITTLE ENGINE THAT COULD.* Most of the hands went up.

Coach Armstrong jumped in and said, *"I think I can, I think I can, I knew I could, I knew I could."*

"That's right," Coach Stackhouse said. "Always believe you can do it. *The body can only achieve what the mind can perceive!"* Then as he pointed to his head he said, "You have to believe to achieve. That is called a positive attitude. We don't want any NMA or negative mental attitudes. That is called 'Stinkin' Thinkin'."

Coach Armstrong took over and said: "Today we are going to work on tackling. In order to do it right, we have to work on the fundamentals. In other words we are going to make it as easy as possible for everyone to understand."

Jason thought, "What can be so difficult about tackling? All you do is just grab the runner and drag him down."

Chapter 8

An Inch Is A Cinch, But A Yard Is Hard

It was only the third day of practice and the players were still dressed in gym clothes, but Coach Stackhouse called them all together to demonstrate tackling. Jason wondered, "How can we practice tackling when we don't even have any equipment?"

Coach Stackhouse had everyone "take a knee" in a semi-circle. Coach Armstrong grabbed a big stand-up dummy that was about five feet tall and just thin enough for a player to get his arms around. As he held it in front of him, Coach Stackhouse spoke to the team. "There are four things that I want you to remember about tackling, ***Dip, Rip, Wrap, and Snap.*** Now everybody say it with me."

All together the players followed Coach's lead, ***"Dip, Rip, Wrap, and Snap."*** He had them repeat it several more times.

He turned to Coach Armstrong and said, "The dummy represents the running back. The first thing a tackler needs to do is to bend his knees. The legs are the most powerful muscles in the body and you need to use them. You tackle with your legs. That is where the 'dip' comes in. You bend your knees and *'Dip'* to get into a good tackling position.

"Look right at the runner's belt buckle; he can't fake you out with that. Keep your head up and slide it to the side so you make contact with the front of your shoulder pad. As you do that, *'Rip'* your arms up and through the runner. Make sure you step into the man and keep driving with your legs.

"*'Wrap'* your arms around him and grasp either your hands or cloth. It is important to grab on and keep your legs going so the runner doesn't spin out or splash off."

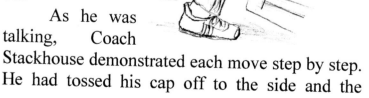

As he was talking, Coach Stackhouse demonstrated each move step by step. He had tossed his cap off to the side and the players could see beads of sweat rolling off his shaved head and dripping from his nose.

Jason noticed every player was watching and **listening with his eyes.** He was impressed how Coach kept his head up and butt down just like he had reminded the players numerous times. Whenever the coach demonstrated, he would stop and check to see that everyone understood what he was saying. Jason liked that. Last year in basketball, Coach Binder used such big words that nobody really knew what was going on.

It was as if Coach was playing freeze tag. He was locked into position with his head up, back arched, butt down, feet apart, and his arms firmly wrapped around the dummy. He held that position as he reviewed the key points, **"Dip, Rip, Wrap, and Snap."**

He paused and then finished by yelling, **"Snap."** As he said, **"Snap,"** he pulled the dummy into him and lifted it up. Still on his feet, he slammed the dummy down saying, "That's how we are going to tackle. Any questions?"

Everyone was so impressed; they just looked at each other speechless. The entire demonstration took only a couple minutes, but the main points were etched in Jason's mind, **"Dip, Rip, Wrap, and Snap!"**

Wiping the sweat from his brow, Coach Stackhouse asked the players, "I forgot to emphasize one key thing that all great tacklers have. Can anyone tell me what it is? Nobody said a word. Just when Coach was going to explain, Brains Brixton's hand shot up.

"Yes, Brent," Coach nodded approvingly. "Tell your teammates."

Brixton replied, "PMA, just like you told us at the first practice."

"Let's have a big clap for Brent," Coach encouraged everyone. "One, two, three, clap!"

Just then Levi chipped in, "Coach, wasn't that the word for today? Attitude? I mean positive mental attitude?"

"You are right Levi; let's give him a clap also. One, two, three..."

Jason thought it was great how the coaches would recognize players with a group clap when they said or did something that deserved recognition.

Coach ended the tackling demonstration by emphasizing how important it was to have a positive mental attitude and believe that you are going to tackle the runner. "We want to have a team meeting at the ball and arrive with an aggressive attitude. *When you are on the football field you want to be Agile, Mobile, and Hostile!"*

The coaches set up a drill where all players had the opportunity to tackle a big dummy held by another player. At first they did it straight on and then from the right and left. As Jason waited in line, the words *"Dip, Rip, Wrap, and Snap"* went through his mind.

Even though Jason wasn't one of the bigger players on the team, he was determined to hit the dummy harder than anyone else. The first time he hit the dummy hard, but forgot to keep driving his legs and the dummy flopped over with Jason on top of it. Coach Armstrong reminded him to lift with the legs as he wrapped his arms.

On his next attempt, Jason kept thinking, "Drive the legs, drive the legs, keep the head up, lift, lift." When his turn came he dipped, ripped, wrapped, lifted, and snapped. It felt good as he slammed the dummy to the ground.

"Vershaw, that's what we like to see, improvement," Coach Armstrong yelled as he patted Jason on the back.

"Wow!" Jason thought. "Coach Armstrong even knows my name."

At the end of practice the entire team started clapping their hands in rhythm with Coach Armstrong. Coach would speed up and slow down. The team followed him like a fine tuned orchestra. Coach stopped with his hands apart and yelled, "Rea-----dy breakdown!"

Everyone yelled, "Hah!" and got into the half-squat "breakdown" position.

Coach started clapping again and repeated the procedure. This time he held the boys in the "breakdown" position and said, "Feel it in your legs; that is where your power comes from! Keep that 'Z' in your knee." Several players started to stand up, but Coach Armstrong reminded them, "Stay down, bend the knees, head up, back arched, butt down, feet apart. That is a good football position."

When Coach could see the boys were getting tired he told them to stand up. "Now that is easy, isn't it? You see why many players like to stand up on the football field? It's easy! To be a good football player you have to bend your knees. We will work on it every day. Anyone can do the easy things right, but to be a good football player you have to do the hard things right. *An inch is a cinch, but a yard is hard!*"

"What did Coach Armstrong mean by that?" Jason wondered as he trotted off the practice field.

Chapter 9

Courage Vs. Fear

Jason looked forward to the ride home on the late bus after practice. His friends Cole and Levi rode the same bus and the ride gave them the opportunity to talk over the events of the day.

Once again, the subject of football practice came up. Levi, with a stocky build, thought he would be an offensive and defensive lineman. Cole, lean and lanky with good speed, was a receiver and defensive back. Jason, with medium build and good quickness was planning to be a running back and linebacker. But, today Coach Armstrong told him he was looking good in the line drills.

"I don't want to be an offensive lineman," Jason told himself. "They never get to carry the ball and don't have any opportunities to score." He pictured himself running down the field on the way to the end zone with defenders bouncing off.

Cole interrupted Jason's daydream with a question. "What do you think Coach Armstrong meant when he said, 'An inch is a cinch, but a yard is hard'?"

Before he could respond, Rocky Swenson, who overheard the question, yelled, "It means stay out of my way or I will squash you like a bug!"

"Nobody asked you," Levi said.

"Well, I'm just saying that I'm looking forward to crunching some people tomorrow," Rocky repeated. "I'm sick of tackling dummies."

Jason, who was the peacemaker, pointed out that Coach was always talking about doing the little things right to make the big things happen. Maybe that's what he meant; it is easy to do the little things, but the big things take more work.

The bus pulled in front of a small ranch style home with a big yard. "This is where I get off," Cole said.

Rocky blocked the aisle, but finally stepped aside when Max, the bus driver, yelled, "Let's go boys!" Cole felt a push in the middle of his backpack as he moved past Rocky. He chose to keep quiet.

Jason thought, "What an idiot!"

In a mocking and threatening voice Rocky yelled, "See you at football practice tomorrow, Christian!"

Within minutes, Jason spotted his home, a remodeled farmhouse with lots of flowers in front and a small orchard off to the side. He greeted his mother, left his backpack on the table and headed out to the garden to check for any new cherry tomatoes. He loved to eat them freshly picked. As he went out the door his mother yelled, "Dinner will be ready in 20 minutes."

While looking for more goodies in the garden, a familiar pickup pulled into the driveway. His dad jumped out of the truck grabbed an old football that was next to the playhouse and yelled, "Go deep!" His dad fired a bomb in a high arc. Jason ran under the ball, but it bounced off his chest to the ground.

"Catch it with your hands," his dad reminded him. Jason threw the ball back, cut to his right, and caught his dad's next pass in full stride – with his hands.

"That's what it's all about," his dad remarked. ***"Keep improving!"*** His dad's job, driving truck, forced him to travel a lot, but he made it a point to spend time with the family when he was home.

Sometimes Jason liked to play catch just for the fun of it, but his dad was always giving him pointers. *"It is easier to learn to do it right than it is to break all your bad habits,"* his dad would say.

Jason's mother called out, "Dinner will be ready in five minutes."

As they walked to the house, his dad asked him, "What did you do at practice today?"

"We were learning how to tackle. Coach had these big dummies that we had to hit and lift backwards."

"How did you do?" his dad inquired.

Jason thought for a second and replied, "I learned how important it is to bend the knees and use the legs. Coach Armstrong says that is where the power comes from."

His dad reminded him to listen to his coach and keep improving. Then he asked, "What are you doing at practice tomorrow?

His mother called, "The food is getting cold."

Jason wanted to tell his dad that he was a little worried about the live tackling drills, but he didn't want him to think he was a wimp.

The next morning Max pulled the big yellow bus in front of the Vershaw house right on time. His cheery, "Good morning kids!" always brightened the day. Jason's sister and little brother ran to beat him on the bus. Since the Vershaw's were the second to last stop, only a few open seats remained.

Jason's heart sank. He had his choice of three seats. Two were next to girls and the other was with Rocky Swenson. He knew the guys would tease him if he sat with one of the girls. Slowly he slipped into the seat next to Rocky.

"How ya doin', Vershaw?" Rocky asked. "Are you ready for the big day?"

Jason, pretending that he didn't know what Rocky was talking about, replied, "Why is this a big day?"

"We finally get to beat up on some people at football practice," Rocky bragged.

"Oh yeah, that's right," Jason agreed. "It will be fun!" He didn't want Rocky to know how worried he really was.

Later at practice, Coach Stackhouse blew his whistle and the players gathered around him in a semi-circle. He always had a few comments to make after the warm-ups were over. "Some of you were a little late getting to practice. I know this is the first day with full pads. It is important to get out to practice on time, so make sure you get to the locker room as soon as possible. We have a lot to do and only an hour and a half to do it."

He told how the coaches made sure every player received the proper size equipment, but he wanted to explain how the helmet should fit. "At first your helmet won't feel very comfortable. It should be snug on the forehead and the cheek pads should fit firmly against the cheeks. If you need larger cheek pads let us know. Notice you have four snaps and all of them must be snapped." He used Stretch Adams, who had a thin face, to show how his cheek pads were much thicker than Tank's.

"When you tackle someone, your helmet shouldn't spin or come down on your nose. If it does, talk with one of the coaches and we will help you."

After more instruction on how to tackle safely, Coach blew his whistle, got everyone's attention, and made a few remarks about the live tackling drills.

"We are going to do some live angle tackling. Everyone will be limited to just two hits, so make them good ones. Remember everything we worked on, head up, aim at the belt buckle, slide the head by in front of the ball carrier, feet apart, back arched, and keep the feet going. Say it with me – **Dip, Rip, Wrap, Snap**."

You could see that Coach was getting more intense as he talked. Then he said something that really got Jason's attention. "It takes courage to be a good tackler. It's normal to be a little nervous before we start the live tackling. It's natural to have a little fear. *Courage is simply putting that fear aside and doing your best. When you do your best, you feel good about yourself.*

"*Courage!* That's the word for today. In order to be a good football player you must be willing to block and tackle. Those are the two most important fundamentals of the game. Both of them require getting after the other person. It takes courage to crash into the opponent and knock him backwards. *Once you get the big hit, you will find this is a real fun game!*"

Chapter 10

The Big Hit

After explaining how to tackle, Coach Stackhouse kept the boys in a semi-circle and he and Coach Armstrong demonstrated how the live tackling drill would run. Stackhouse put two practice vests on the ground about ten yards apart. He then placed another vest on the ground in the middle five yards from each vest.

He instructed the players that they would be in two rows lined up behind the vests facing each other. On the coaches' signal, the offensive player would run toward the middle vest. When he got to the middle vest, he would cut either right or left. The defensive man would wait until the ball carrier made his cut, then attack to make the tackle.

The tackler would keep good tackling form and drive his head past in front of the ball carrier. Coach emphasized that it is more important for the tackler to keep his feet and drive the runner backward instead of taking him down. The runner was instructed to make only one cut and not try to fake out the tackler. "Remember," Coach Armstrong said, "this is a tackling drill. We want to help the defensive man learn how to tackle."

They demonstrated the drill with Coach Stackhouse tackling Coach Armstrong. After the tackle, Armstrong reviewed the key steps for the players.

"OK, now it is your turn," Coach Stackhouse said. "Find a player about your size." After the players partnered up, he split them in two groups and sent half with Coach Armstrong.

"Ha!" Jason thought, "Rocky isn't even in my group. I don't have to worry about being 'crunched' by him." Rocky and Tank were matched up and sent to Coach Armstrong's area.

Jason's partner was Cole Christian. He was about the same weight and a friend. Jason didn't want Cole to show him up.

Jason got in the tackling line and Cole in the runner line. Jason was happy several players were ahead of him so he could watch how they did. The first couple of tacklers weren't very aggressive and Coach Armstrong yelled that he wanted to "hear the hit." Jason reviewed in his mind, "Dip, Rip, Wrap, Snap," then he repeated Coach's words, "Hit, Hit, Hit!"

As Jason's turn approached, he had the feeling that everyone was watching him and he wanted to make a good impression. When Cole got the ball, Jason's feet started chopping and it felt like his heart was going to jump out of his chest. He remembered Coach's comment, "The most aggressive player will win."

Cole tucked the ball under his arm and made a cut at the vest. Jason bit down hard on his mouth guard and moved in aggressively for the tackle. He felt like he was shot out of a cannon. Bracing himself for the collision, Jason closed his eyes, dropped his head, and flew right past the runner. He got a piece of Cole with his arm, but couldn't wrap and snap because the runner just spun him around and kept going.

He dreaded Coach's comments. "Vershaw, I like your enthusiasm and aggressiveness, but you have got to stay under control. Keep your head up and eyes open. You've got to see what you are going to hit. *"Keep your eyes on the prize."*

Jason was embarrassed. He had heard of an air ball, but never an air tackle.

Now it was his turn to carry the ball and Cole was the tackler. Still thinking about his failure to tackle, he approached the vest and made a slow cut to his right. Not concentrating on protecting himself, Jason was straight up and down and wasn't prepared for the tackle. Cole drove his shoulder into Jason's exposed midsection. Jason stumbled backward, the ball went flying, and he fell flat on his back. As he was gasping for breath, he looked up and saw

Coach Stackhouse down on one knee looking into his eyes.

Coach encouraged him to, "Relax and take deep, slow breaths. You got the wind knocked out of you. You'll be all right in just a minute." Sure enough, once Jason relaxed he caught his breath and got back up.

"Sorry about that," Cole said to Jason.

Jason thought, "Boy that was a big hit!" Each player had another chance to tackle, but Jason just went through the motions on his final attempt. It seemed that he never really recovered from Cole's big hit.

After the live tackling drills the coaches called all the players together in a semi-circle. Coach Stackhouse explained that it takes awhile to get the fundamentals down. He asked whoever felt they had a good tackle to raise his hand. Out of 38 players, only six raised their hand: Bobby Benson, Levi Carter, Juan Gomez, and Seth Thomas. Jason could understand those four; they were all considered good athletes, but he really wondered about Rocky and Tank. They had their hands up high and Coach Armstrong asked, "Are you sure you fellas should have your hands up?"

They sheepishly dropped their hands as Coach Stackhouse asked Coach Armstrong, "What did you think of the first live tackling?"

Armstrong commented, "We have a lot of work to do. The big thing is to keep improving. I like how the boys are listening and doing what the coaches tell them. Most everyone had trouble with tackling for the first time. *What's important is not how good you are now, but how good you can become."*

"All good points Coach," Stackhouse said. *"You always want to be better than you were yesterday, but not as good as you will be tomorrow."*

  That night sitting at the table for dinner, Jason's dad asked, "Well, buddy, did you get that 'big hit' today?"

  Jason rubbed his side and replied, "Yes, I sure did."

Chapter 11

Respect Everyone: Fear No One

It was the tenth day of practice and Jason and his teammates were preparing for tomorrow's big scrimmage with Coon Creek, a neighboring school. After scrimmaging the Wildcats, they would play five games in the Northeastern Middle School Conference.

Over the years, the Scenic Valley Eagles had built a reputation for being one of the most competitive teams in the six-team league. Last year's record was three and two, and both losses were by close scores.

Several times Coach Stackhouse told the players not to be concerned about winning or losing. He encouraged each individual to concentrate on playing his best and working together as a team and the wins would happen. Coach had a way of saying things that got a person's attention. For example: "Don't watch the scoreboard, you don't control it, but you do control the way you play. *Focus on what you can control!"*

Since the first day of live tackling, Jason's confidence level had increased considerably. He was getting the idea of staying under control when tackling and was adjusting to playing in the offensive line.

At first, he was disappointed when the coaches moved him to offensive guard. He wanted to be a running back just like his dad. Jason knew he was one of the faster players on the team, but Coach Stackhouse said the team needed quickness at the guard positions. He explained the offense required the guards to pull and lead on the sweeps and Jason had just the right size and quickness for the position.

It just happened to be the day Jason was moved into the line when the word-of-the-day was *"Pride."* Coach Armstrong told the team that pride in your performance means that you expect to do your best on each play. He also spoke of *"Team Pride."* That is when he stated the team was more important than the individual. He went on to say, *"There is no I in T-E-A-M! It's not about me, it's about WE!"*

Jason was starting to like playing guard. He lined up between Brains, who was at center, and Rocky at tackle. He thought it was strange that he and Rocky never got along, but now that they were playing next to each other, they were actually becoming friends. Since he had been out for football, Jason was making many new friends. It seems like when you work hard at practice and sweat together you learn to respect each other.

It was a hot, muggy day, and several of the players were loafing and dragging butt when the coaches gave the team a water break. Coach Armstrong had been demonstrating taking the proper pursuit angle and had worked up quite a sweat. *"Be a tackler, don't be a chaser,"* he yelled as he demonstrated how to cut off the running back. *"Never run around a block. Go across the face of the blocker - that's where the ball carrier will be."*

Coach's T-shirt with a big Scenic Valley Eagle on the front and the words *"Play with Pride"* was soaked with sweat. It seemed like he was always coaching on the run and expected the players to *"hustle"* right along with him. As he bent forward to address the team, little rivers of sweat were running down his neck changing the color of his shirt from light gray to dark gray.

He wiped his hand across his brow and held it in front of the team. It was dripping with sweat. He asked the team, "What is this?"

About half the team yelled, "Sweat!"

"That's right," he replied. Then he asked, "Where does it come from?" Before anyone could say anything, he answered his own question. "It comes from inside - it's an inside job! You have to earn it! You can't walk into the store and lay down a dollar bill and say, 'I want to buy a quart of sweat.' It just doesn't work that way. ***You can't buy sweat!*** You must earn it. When you sweat, remember, it is because you are giving an all out effort. You are earning it. And you are doing it for the team! That's what this great game is all about."

"Wow!" Jason thought. "That really fired up the team. It seemed like everyone just forgot about the heat and had fun practicing."

After practice, Coach Stackhouse explained the purpose of the scrimmage. "This gives us the opportunity to go against some different competition. For the past couple weeks we have been practicing against each other. The starting line-ups for the first game will not be determined until after the scrimmage. Everyone will have the opportunity to play. The coaches will be evaluating your performance."

"Coon Creek is well-coached and they have a good team. I want everyone to have a high degree of ***class.*** By that I mean ***concentrate on your performance,*** no trash talking or talking back to the referees. Remember, the officials will enforce the rules and make sure everything goes smoothly. Listen to them and learn from them. After the game we will shake hands with the opponent and congratulate them on a good scrimmage."

The coaches even demonstrated how to shake hands, how to act after scoring (hand the ball to the official), and what to do in case of an injury.

Coach Stackhouse concluded his comments by telling the team: ***"Respect every one, fear no one!*** As the season goes on, we will prepare for each team as if they are undefeated and we are zero and zero. At the same time we will go into each game believing we will win. The coaching staff will have you well prepared. It is up to each of you to play to the best of your ability."

Chapter 12

Scrimmage Time

The scrimmage was scheduled for 10:00 AM Saturday at the Eagles' practice field. Jason had trouble sleeping Friday night. Even though it was just a scrimmage, he wanted to do well and was still a bit nervous about competing against another school. Coon Creek was a bigger school and he expected they would have a huge team.

Jason's parents heard him moving around in his room much earlier than usual. Normally on Saturday morning he would sleep in and wouldn't be up and around until his mother called him about 9:00. Realizing he was pretty worked up about the scrimmage, Jason's mom went upstairs to his room to check on him.

"Is everything OK?" she asked as she knocked on his door.

"Yeah, I'm all right," he replied.

"Can I come in?" his mother questioned.

"Sure, come on in."

"What seems to be the problem?"

"Nothing."

His mother decided to bring up the topic. "I bet it has to do with the scrimmage this morning."

"Well, I guess so. You know this is my first tackle scrimmage ever. What if I mess up?"

His mother probed a little more. "Jason, you like football, don't you?"

"I guess so."

"You talk a lot about it and I know you have made many new friends. Why don't you just approach the scrimmage like you are going out to have fun with your friends?"

"I guess you're right Mom, but sometimes I worry about what might go wrong."

His mother reminded him that they had discussed this topic once before. She then asked, "And what did we decide?"

"I know, I should concentrate on what will go right instead of what might go wrong. But, sometimes that is hard to do."

His mother recalled what Jason shared with her a week or so ago. "Remember when Coach Stackhouse told the team that, 'Sometimes you have to do the things that are hard to do'?"

Jason's eyes seemed to light up and his mother could see that she made a connection.

He thought for a moment and said, "I'll be OK. I'm just a little nervous."

"Remember, it's OK to be nervous. I'll fix a good breakfast. While I'm getting it ready you can feed the dogs."

By talking it over with his mom, Jason felt relieved. As he filled the dog dishes he thought, ***"Courage is what it takes to overcome fear."***

Jason was one of the first players to report to the locker room. He took his time getting his uniform on. The rest of the team gradually drifted in. Brains was also in early, and Jason checked with him on a few plays. For the scrimmage, the coaches had put in three running plays to the right and four to the left, along with three pass plays.

"Hey Brains," Jason asked, "I know I pull to lead the blocking on 48 Sweep Right, but what if I have a lineman on me and you are covered with a lineman too?"

"Jason, just remember your rule; you pull on 48 Sweep Right regardless of what defense they are in."

"But who will block the player on me?"

"Rocky, at right tackle, blocks the first man to his inside. Stretch, the tight end, blocks the first man to his inside, and Devin, the wingback, blocks the first man to his inside. You see, everybody blocks down to the inside and you pull to block the first man to the outside. If you don't

pull, the outside man won't get blocked. The fullback fakes up the middle so he can't block outside."

It was great to have Brixton at center because he was so intelligent that he knew everybody's responsibility on every play.

Brains knew things came a little more difficult to Jason. Once again, he reminded him, "Don't worry about what defense they are in, just remember your blocking rules."

Coach Armstrong yelled, "We are going to take the field in five minutes."

As Jason was going over the plays with Brains, the other players were getting dressed and he didn't realize how close they were to scrimmage time. He was hoping they would get to run the 33 Trap. Coach Armstrong said they put it in just for him. It gave him the opportunity to pull flat down the line to his left and block out the first player to show. It was a great block because Brixton and the left guard, Bobby Markins, double-teamed the nose guard. Tank Tankson, the left tackle, blocked the linebacker to the inside and that left the defensive tackle unblocked. That is when Jason would sneak past the double team and lay a surprise kick-out block on the defensive tackle. They ran it a couple times in practice and it worked perfectly.

Even though it was just a scrimmage and no score would be kept, Jason was excited about being in the starting offensive lineup on the Red Team. The coaches reminded them that the lineups could change, but on the bulletin board next to Coach Stackhouse's office, the three teams were posted as Red, White and Blue. Coach told the team there was no official "first team," but everyone knew the Red Team was the best one. Jason beamed as he saw his name

Red Team

LE	LT	LG	Center	RG	RT	RE
Christian	Tankson	Markins	Brixton	Vershaw	Swenson	Adams
			QB			**WB**
			Komp			Young
	TB		**FB**			
	Benson		Carter			

posted right up there with Bobby's and Rocky's.

Jason was determined to keep his spot at right guard with the Red Team. On defense, he was on the White Team right behind Leon Stevens. The coaches told the players that no one would start on both sides of the ball. Coach Stackhouse often said, "Everyone who makes all the practices, works hard, listens to the coaches, and makes a commitment to the team will play in the games."

Prior to the scrimmage, Coach Armstrong put the linemen through some blocking drills while Coach Stackhouse worked with the backs. Even though the coaches were going to concentrate on the running game during the scrimmage, Devin Komp and James Schlies, the top two quarterbacks, threw some passes to the backs and ends. Eventually the coaches brought the team together and ran some offensive plays.

Since it was a scrimmage, there was no kicking or punting. Each team would get the ball on their 40-yard line and have 15 offensive plays. Jason was looking forward to getting started, yet at the same time he was unsure about how he would do. Coach blew his whistle and yelled, "Red Offense."

Chapter 13

Persistence: The Key To
Success

Coach Stackhouse gathered the Red Offense together for a few words of encouragement before Brixton took his place over the ball on the 40-yard line.

"Boys, we have been practicing for two weeks against ourselves. Now is the time to come together as a team and show what we can do. Let them know from the first snap that we came to play aggressive football. On the first play hit that player across from you as hard as you can. That will set the tempo for the day.

"We are going to start with a 31 Fullback Dive and then we will run a 48 Sweep Right. Remember, the Dive is all straight blocking so really get after the player across from you. Let's get at least five yards."

Jason thought it was neat that the coaches could be on the field and in the huddle to help them out with any questions. The plays were setup so they were easy to understand. Each lineman had a number with even to the right of center and odd to the left. The backs also had a number from one to four, so if the play was a sweep around right end it was a 48 Sweep. That meant the "4" back would run through the "8" hole.

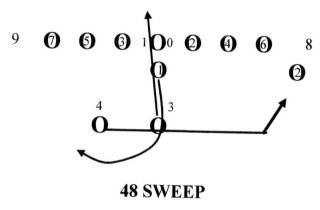

48 SWEEP

One play would look like another. When the Eagles ran 31 FB Dive, they faked the 48 Sweep Right, and when they ran the 48 Sweep they faked the Fullback Dive. Because of that, the coaches emphasized good faking by the backs and quarterback.

The 31 FB Dive and the 48 Sweep had the same backfield action, but for the linemen it was much different. On the Dive play Jason fired out to block the linebacker. He remembered Coach Armstrong's coaching tip, "Always anticipate movement. Aim where the defender will be, not where he is." Coach knew Jason liked to go pheasant hunting with his dad so he reminded him, "When you are bird hunting you have to shoot where the bird is going to be, not where it is. If you shoot where the bird is, you will hit where it was. That is why the linemen should always know where the back will be running."

Jason got a good piece of the LB. Levi took the ball and pounded up the middle behind Bobby Markins and Brixton.

"Great job linemen!" Coach Armstrong shouted as he returned to the huddle. "We will take the five yards. Now let's run the 48 Sweep."

The sweep was one of Jason's favorite plays because he got to pull out and block on the outside where he had a chance to spring the running back for a big gain.

As he pulled around end, Jason spotted a small cornerback coming up to make the play. He thought, "OK, I'm going to really blast him." Jason accelerated to make the block; the defender stepped to the side and used his hands to push Jason to the ground. Bobby Benson got hit for a three-yard loss

"Shoot," Jason said to himself. "It was all my fault." He hung his head as he headed back to the huddle.

Coach Armstrong put his hand on Jason's shoulder as he returned to the huddle. "Remember, stay under control, widen your base, drop your butt, and keep your head up. You will get him next time. *That play is over. There is nothing you can do about it now, so look forward to the next play."*

As Coach Stackhouse was calling the next play, Jason heard his dad's voice, "Jason, keep your head up!"

Jason felt embarrassed. He was happy that his parents supported him. They were usually at his activities, but he wished that his dad would just let him play without trying to coach.

It was a good scrimmage for the Scenic Valley Eagles. When it was over the coaches told them that they learned a lot about the team and they were pleased with the overall effort. Everyone did get the opportunity to play, even Matthew Mulroy who was the smallest boy in the seventh grade.

Jason felt pretty good about the way he played on offense. Even though he missed a couple blocks on the sweep, he knew all his plays and had a couple really good blocks on the 33 Trap. The first time they ran the trap Jason pulled across the center to block the defender to be trapped and Tank was standing right in the hole. Jason ran into Tank and the FB got hit for a loss.

Coach Armstrong was pretty worked up and everybody heard him yell, "Tankson, if you don't know what to do – ASK! How many times do I have to tell you that?" In fact, after about ten plays Coach replaced him with Moose Mullen. Moose didn't have a lot of athletic ability, but he did know his plays.

Jason learned several things from the scrimmage. He knew that it was important to put out a great effort, but he began to realize he had to play under control. Coach Stackhouse called it, ***"Playing hard, but also playing smart."*** He also learned that when he made a mistake it was best to forget about it and go on to the next play. Like Coach Armstrong said, ***"The most important play is the one coming up next."***

After the scrimmage, Jason sat on the bench in front of his locker. He tucked his dirty clothes in his gym bag and carefully hung up his equipment. He looked around to make sure he didn't leave any socks or other gear on the floor. The coaches preached that real winners leave the locker room clean. In his mind he could hear Coach Stackhouse reminding the team after practice: "Think of others; pick up after yourself. If you don't pick it up someone else will have to."

Coach was always the last one out of the locker room. If he found unclaimed gear or dirt dragged in, the team ran laps. It didn't take long for the players to get in the habit of keeping the locker room clean.

The family stopped at Dairy Queen for a treat to celebrate Jason's big day. He ordered a Snickers Blizzard, which was special since his parents seldom allowed him to have one. Tank and his parents were sitting in a booth toward the back. Jason went back to say hello and found that Tank was upset.

"I hardly got to play any offense," Tank complained.

"Yeah," Tank's dad said, "I told him he might as well quit."

Just then, Jason's dad arrived and patted Tank on the back as he said, "Nice job today. I saw you make a couple good tackles."

Tank's dad, who never played organized sports asked, "Did you hear the coach yell at him? Right in front of the entire team! That wasn't necessary. He might as well quit."

Jason's dad replied, "I think Tank has a lot of potential. Maybe the coach was just trying to impress on him how important it is for Tank to know what to do on every play. *When the coach yells at a player that means he sees some potential and wants that player to get better.* If a player makes a mistake and the coach doesn't say anything, that usually means he has given up on him."

Somewhat startled, Tank's dad said, "Really! I never looked at it that way. Maybe Tank should stay with it."

"Absolutely!" Jason's dad agreed. ***"You know in sports there are many ups and downs and you really find out what you are made of when things don't go right.*** It's easy to have a great attitude when everything is going terrific. Life is kind of like the game of football, you have to learn to get up and go again after getting knocked down. *It's all about persistence!"*

"Hey Tank," Jason said, "Rocky and Brains and some other linemen are coming over to my house tomorrow to go over our offensive plays. Why don't you join us?"

Cheering up a bit, Tank replied, "I'll think about it."

Chapter 14

Honesty: The Best Policy

On Monday, after the big scrimmage, the word spread fast through the seventh grade. The starting line-ups for the opening game with the Roselawn Wolves were posted on Coach Stackhouse's door. The coaches said they would name the starting teams on Monday so the players would have the opportunity to work together for a full week.

Jason, Cole, and Levi headed down to Coach's office prior to their first hour class. Jason knew he missed a number of blocks in the scrimmage. He also felt he showed improvement as the scrimmage progressed. In fact, Coach Armstrong spoke with him after the scrimmage and told him that he "liked his attitude." He told Jason that he was always hustling and listening to the coaches. Coach assured him, "Keep it up and you will play a lot of football this year."

In spite of Coach Armstrong's comments, Jason was afraid he might not be in the starting lineup.

In bold letters, Coach had the starting lineups posted in the window of his office door.

Starting Offense vs. Roselawn

LE	LT	LG	Center	RG	RT	RE
Christian	Mullen	Markins	Brixton	Vershaw	Swenson	Adams
			QB			**WB**
			Komp			Young
	TB		**FB**			
	Benson		Carter			

Jason's eyes darted to the right guard position. He tried to hide his excitement when he saw the name "Vershaw" on the sheet.

Christian was the first to speak, "Look at left tackle. Moose has moved in ahead of Tank. I bet Tank will quit now."

"Wait a minute," Jason said. "Did you look at the starting defense? They moved Tank to starting defensive tackle."

Levi piped in, "He doesn't have to remember as much on defense."

"He did make some good tackles on defense. He will be real tough to move off the line," added Jason.

As excited as he was when he saw his name listed with the starting offense, Jason was disappointed when he saw the defensive starters.

Starting Defense vs. Roselawn

		Safety Rynders	**Safety** Gomez		
CB Sommers		**LB** King	**LB** Thomas		**CB** Rico
DE Steltz	**DT** Tankson	**Nose** Grimm	**DT** Sievert	**DE** Volkman	

The boys quickly noticed that no one was starting both ways. Not even Bobby Benson or Devin Komp. Levi let everybody know that he could play linebacker better than Seth Thomas. Jason spoke up in Seth's defense, "Levi, you are starting at fullback and the coaches told us they plan to play as many players as possible. You will see plenty of action."

Levi was one of the most aggressive players on the team and didn't want to sit out on defense. But after talking it over with his teammates, he realized Seth had been working hard in practice and deserved to play. He accepted it better when he noticed he was listed at second team LB, backing up Thomas. "I hope I get to play some defense," Levi told Jason.

Just when everything was really going great for Jason he was confronted with a problem. All seventh graders were required to take an introduction to foreign language class. Jason selected Spanish along with a number of his teammates. Usually a B to B+ student, Jason found the class difficult. Some of the other students had been exposed to Spanish in another class, but for Jason this was his first experience.

Miss Kohler, the teacher, was a tall, thin woman with tight curly hair. She was friendly enough and had many interesting class activities, but Jason had trouble with the vocabulary. Most of the time she spoke Spanish in class and usually Jason was lost. He knew he wasn't doing very well and when the next big test came up he managed to sneak a peek at Brent "Brains" Brixton's paper. Jason told Brains he was struggling and asked if he would help him out by keeping the last page uncovered on his desk. In fact, Jason copied the entire vocabulary page.

When he got his paper back, he had numerous mistakes on the first two pages, but the last page was perfect. On top of the third page Miss Kohler wrote, "Jason, see me after class."

Jason respected Miss Kohler. She even went out of her way to give him extra help. Having a reputation for having high standards, several times prior to the test she reminded the students to do their own work.

He knew he was in trouble. It was difficult for him to concentrate during the rest of the class as he struggled for a reasonable explanation.

Then he decided he would tell her that he really studied hard and was pleased with the results.

It seemed like the class would never get over; finally the tone sounded and he sheepishly walked up to Miss Kohler's desk.

"You wanted me to see you after class?" Jason asked.

"Yes," Miss Kohler replied. "I see that you did perfectly on the vocabulary part of the test. How do you feel about the last page?"

Jason swallowed hard and said, "Good, really good. I studied the vocabulary for over an hour last night!"

"Is there anything else you want to tell me?" she asked.

"No, not really," he answered.

On his way to the lunchroom Jason's stomach was upset. He knew he lied to Miss Kohler and didn't feel very good about it. "Oh well, maybe I will feel better after lunch," he thought as he took his place in line.

Jason was one of the last students to go through the hot lunch line. He took his tray and sat down with Justin Keller and Stretch Adams.

"What did Curley Kohler want?" Justin asked.

"Ooh, she wanted to congratulate me on how well I did on the vocabulary part of the test."

"What did you get?" Justin inquired.

"I had them all right!" Jason said with a certain amount of pride in his voice.

"Who did you copy from?" Justin questioned.

Jason defended himself with another lie. "I didn't copy. I studied and did my own work."

Just then, Jason made eye contact with Brains Brixton who was seated at the end of the table. Apparently, he overheard the talk and gave Jason a dirty look.

The tone sounded and the boys moved on to their next class. Brains caught up with Jason in the hall and said, "Keep me out of it. I didn't have anything to do with your vocab test."

After school, as he was heading out to practice, Jason thought, "Boy, I sure hope Miss Kohler believed me. I don't want to deal with any more questions."

Then he wondered, "Why did she ask me if I had anything else that I wanted to tell her?"

Coach Stackhouse blew his whistle. The players jogged a lap around the goalpost and came back into formation for flexibility drills. Following the exercises, the team formed a semi-circle around Coach Stackhouse for the cadence drill and some inspirational words. He finished his comments with the word of the day.

"Today's word is **'Honesty.'** Be honest with your coaches, with your teammates, and yourself. The best way to never be caught lying is to always tell the truth. It is a lot easier to live with yourself when you are truthful. *It takes a lifetime to build a reputation, but only one incident to destroy it.* The best way to tell if you're being honest with yourself is to look into the mirror and do a self-evaluation. You can fool other people, but you can't fool yourself."

Coach directed the defensive linemen to go with Coach Armstrong. Jason joined the DB's and LB's to work on pass defense. As he ran to the far end of the field, Coach Stackhouse's words echoed in his mind. *"It takes a lifetime to build a reputation, but only one incident to destroy it."*

Chapter 15

Commitment: "You Can Count On Me."

Practice was going great. Jason was working on his defensive pass drop. Coach Armstrong complimented him several times for his footwork and ability to drop into underneath coverage.

"Keep your head on a swivel," Coach yelled as he encouraged the linebackers to look for any receivers as they dropped into their pass defense zones. At the seventh grade level most passes were hooks, curls, or crossing patterns and it was important for the linebackers to play pass defense. Jason was coached to defend the run first, but if he saw the QB passing, to get depth and look for someone coming into his zone.

Blitzing was not allowed in middle school football. Often the QB had quite a bit of time to pass and Coach knew the Wolves had an excellent quarterback. Several of the players played basketball and baseball against T. D. Kraft, the Roselawn quarterback. He was a talented three-sport athlete and they were aware he was a threat whether passing or running. Coach Armstrong knew in order to beat the Wolves they needed to contain Kraft.

After several tackling and pursuit drills, the players were given a water break while the coaches prepared for special teams. Everyone on the team was involved in special teams in some way. Some middle school leagues didn't include punting and kicking, but Coach Stackhouse was pleased that their league did. He agreed the more fundamentals that could be taught at the early grades, the better it was for the future.

Jason was a member of the punting team and the kickoff team. He was particularly pleased when Coach Armstrong set up the kickoff team and said, "We need the most aggressive players to be on kickoff coverage. Vershaw, I want you to be one of the 'Missile Men' right next to the kicker. Your job is to run as fast as you can downfield and bust up any blocking that is setting up. If you make the tackle that's better yet! Can you do that for the team?"

"You can count on me Coach!" Jason replied.

"That's what I like," Coach Armstrong said. *"Commitment!* No excuses, and I **am** counting on you!"

Jason thought, "A couple weeks ago I didn't know if I would like to mix it up and now I'm the 'Missile Man' on the kickoff team. Wow!"

Next Coach Armstrong said, "I need an outside contain man on the left side to take the place of Benson." Bobby Benson was the starting tailback, and he was returning punts and kickoffs so Coach decided to replace him on the kickoff team.

"How about you, Summers?" Coach asked. Dustin Summers had good speed and made a few impressive tackles in the scrimmage. He also started at cornerback. "How about it? Can you handle that left side contain position?"

Dustin said, "I'll try."

Coach Armstrong put his hand on Dustin's shoulder, looked into his eyes and said, "Try? What does that mean? *We don't need someone to try. We need someone who will do it! Can we count on you to make a commitment?*"

"I will do it. You can count on me," Sommers remarked.

At the conclusion of practice, Coach Stackhouse gathered the team together and reminded them that they had only four more practices before their Saturday morning game with Roselawn. He stressed how important it was to know all their responsibilities on every play.

"During most games we run about forty offensive plays. If we have only one mistake at each position that makes a total of eleven mistakes. In other words, one out of every four plays will be messed up. Before you leave the locker room tonight, pick up a play list from Coach Armstrong. He has the 5-2 defense diagrammed on the sheet against our offensive set. Draw out your responsibility on each play and then check the back of the sheet to see if you are right. Now be honest, and do it without peeking at the answers."

Bobby led the team in a "breakdown" to conclude practice. The boys were taking off their shoes and going into the locker room when Brains asked Jason, "Do you know all of your plays?"

Jason said, "Yes, I've got them all down!"

"Great," Brains replied. "Then you won't need my help."

"What did he mean by that?" Jason asked himself. "I think he is referring back to Spanish class. I wish I would never have asked him to let me see his paper."

The team now had four running plays to the right and four to the left. Coach added another pass play to give the Eagles a total of twelve plays.

91

After supper, Jason sat at his desk, took out the play list, and unfolded it in front of him. At the top it said, "Eagle Offense Vs. 5-2 Defense." He had six different diagrams with all the plays listed at the bottom.

Eagle Offense Vs. 5-2 Defense

```
        V                   V

V               V       V               V
    V   V       V       V   V
    O   O   O   O   O   O   O
                O                   O

        O           O
```

31 Dive	30 Dive	30 Dive Pass
48 Sweep	33 Trap	34 Power Pass
27 Counter Trap	29 Sweep	Pop Pass
32 Wham	34 Power	29 Boot Pass

The coaches liked to have the players draw up the plays along with their responsibility on each play. Coach Stackhouse encouraged the linemen to know the backfield action and the backs to know what the linemen were doing. Jason could hear Coach Armstrong's words echo, "There is a much better chance for success when you know your responsibility and the job of the player on either side of you."

Jason knew that Brains had down every lineman's assignment on every play. He figured if Brains could do that, he could at least know his and the players' next to him.

Most of the plays were easy to remember. If the play was a "Dive" or "Power" to his side of the line, he would fire out and block the man on him away from the hole. Since the "Sweeps" were two of the first plays coach put in, he was confident on them. As he drew the plays out he had trouble on one – the 29 Boot Pass. He remembered it was a fake 29 Sweep, but he couldn't remember if he had to pull.

He wanted to look at the answer on the back of the sheet, but he remembered Coach Armstrong saying, "Draw them all in first and then go back and check. That is the **honest** thing to do." He followed Coach's instructions and

eventually determined he needed to study the 29 Bootleg a little more.

After an hour or so of working on his plays, Jason was confident that he had fulfilled his *commitment* to his coaches and the team. He knew what to do and the Eagles could *count on him to do his best on every play.*

Just then he heard his mother's footsteps coming up the stairs. He quickly tucked away his football sheet and started working on his math assignment.

"How's the homework coming?" his mother asked.

"Good," Jason replied.

His mother said, "Finish up soon; it's almost bedtime!"

"OK, Mom."

Before he began to concentrate on his math assignment, Jason decided to take one more look at the play list and the football diagrams.

He saw something that he hadn't seen before. At the bottom of the sheet Coach Armstrong asked a question, "Do you remember the word of the day for each practice?" He added four columns with three words in each column.

Team	*Courage*	*Hustle*	*Concentration*
Pride	*Respect*	*Class*	*Responsibility*
Attitude	*Belief*	*Commitment*	*Honesty*

How are you doing on these?

Chapter 16

The Truth Wins Out

Jason was awakened by the sounds of his older sister and younger brother scurrying around getting ready for school. He was still tired. No matter what he did he just couldn't get comfortable in bed. He'd stayed up late completing his math homework. He kept thinking about Coach Armstrong's message on the back of his play sheet. "How are you doing on these?" He couldn't help but notice the last word was the word of the day for yesterday – *"Honesty."*

He thought, "I wasn't honest with Miss Kohler and then I wasn't very honest with my mom. But I have been honest with the coaches and the team. I've been working hard, doing my best, and I know all of the plays. Oh, I wish school was as much fun as football. I wish I could do my homework like I can work on my football plays. I don't want to go to Spanish class today. Maybe I'm getting sick. But if I miss school, I won't be able to go to football practice. How can I tell Miss Kohler that I'm sorry that I copied the vocab part of the test?"

"Jason, are you up?" his mother called.

"I'll be right down Mom."

His mother noticed that Jason seemed preoccupied. She asked him, "Jason, you're awfully quiet this morning. Is everything OK?"

"Yeah, I'm all right! I'm just a little tired."

Max pulled the big yellow bus up in front of the Vershaw house. Tyler gave him a hardy hello and Cheyenne responded with a big grin and a, "Good morning Max!"

"Hello Jason! Max flashed a quick smile.

"Yeah, right," Jason replied.

Max looked confused. Usually Jason was very cheerful.

First hour English class was a drag. Second hour math was OK. "At least I got a 90% on my math homework," Jason thought.

It was difficult to concentrate in third hour science because Jason had fourth hour Spanish on his mind.

Miss Kohler was at her usual spot next to the classroom door. She greeted all the students with a hello and a welcoming smile.

"Good morning Bobby, hello Miranda, looking good this morning Justin." She liked to call the students by name as she welcomed them to the classroom.

Jason was uncertain as he approached the room. "Maybe I can just sneak in without her noticing me," he thought.

"Hi Jason!" Miss Kohler offered her usual friendly greeting.

"Good morning," Jason replied. Then he thought, "Gee, she spoke to me just like she always does, maybe everything will be OK."

Spanish class started with Miss Kohler telling the class that they were going to have a fifteen-minute period to complete a word usage "funsheet." Most teachers called them "worksheets," but Miss Kohler told the students when you have been doing your regular assignments the classwork would be fun.

She passed out the "funsheets," but when she got to Jason she quietly said, "Complete this first."

Jason looked at the paper for a few seconds, and realized it contained the same vocabulary words as yesterday, but they were in a different order. He just froze as he stared at the sheet. Jason only knew about half of the words. What would he do? Then he thought about what his parents had told him many times. He also thought back to yesterday's football practice and Coach Stackhouse's comments.

He knew there was only one thing he could do. ***He had to tell the truth and accept responsibility for his actions.*** It took a lot of *courage,* but on the top of his paper he wrote:

"I copied yesterday's answers. I'm sorry."

He walked his paper up to Miss Kohler's desk and handed it to her. She took the paper, glanced at it, and gave him the day's funsheet.

Jason actually had a feeling of relief. Miss Kohler had a great activity planned for the day and Jason got into it. He pretty much forgot about his situation until the end of class when he was leaving the room. Miss Kohler stopped him and said, "Jason, stop by my room after school."

Jason said, "I have football practice after school."

Miss Kohler informed him, "I have spoken with Coach Armstrong and told him that you would be late for practice."

"I'm in big trouble," Jason thought as he walked down the hall toward the lunchroom.

It was "Taco Tuesday," usually one of Jason's favorite meals, but he couldn't even taste his food. Many questions ran through his mind

"How would he explain this to the team? What will the coaches say? What will Miss Kohler do? What if his parents find out?"

Jason concluded the obvious. "I should have done my own work and I wouldn't have this problem."

He didn't say much to his friends. Jason wanted to get the school day over and head out to football practice where he could forget about Spanish class.

The walk from his school locker to the Spanish room seemed twice as long as normal. He passed Rocky who said, "Jason, you're going the wrong way."

Brains glanced at him and managed a feeble, "Good luck Jason."

Jason walked into Miss Kohler's room and felt like the weight of the entire universe was on his shoulders. Miss Kohler was sitting at her desk and on the other side of the desk sat Jason's mother.

"I'm very disappointed in you," his mother said.

His chin was on his chest and he was fighting back tears.

Miss Kohler told him to sit down on a chair next to his mother. "What do you have to say for yourself?" she asked.

"I'm sorry, I made a mistake," he muttered. "It won't happen again."

Miss Kohler gave him some extra work to do. She added, "This isn't punishment, these papers will help you learn the vocabulary words. Turn them in tomorrow. But, you will get a zero on your test."

"One more question, did Brent know you were copying or did you do it without his knowledge?"

"Oh no!" Jason thought, "I was hoping she wouldn't ask that question. I can't rat on one of my friends."

"What role did Brent play?" she repeated the question.

"Well, I guess he kinda knew," Jason acknowledged, "it was like he didn't cover up his answers."

Miss Kohler could see Jason was uncomfortable and getting worked up, so she decided to drop that line of questioning and move on.

After more discussion and a promise from Jason that he had learned his lesson, Jason and his mother got up to leave. His mother shook hands with Miss Kohler and assured her that in the future Jason would be doing his best in class.

Miss Kohler put her hand on Jason's shoulder and remarked, "This incident is over. Tomorrow is a new day and you start with a clean slate." She smiled, shook his hand, and said,

"What's done is done. Let's have a great rest of the school year."

"Mom, I've got to get to practice," Jason wailed.

"Jason, there will be no football practice tonight. You are going home with me to finish your school work." In spite of Jason pleading with her, his mother remained firm. "No practice!"

Missing practice was bad enough, but now he had to face his dad. Jason's father was a soft-hearted, but very disciplined man. He had high values and expected his children to live up to them. Miss Kohler had called home the night before and explained the situation, so Jason's dad knew what was going on.

After dinner he sat down and had a talk with his father. His dad remained calm, but explained that Jason made a mistake and *now he had to accept the consequences of his actions. He emphasized that the most important thing was that he learned from the incident and that he becomes a better person as a result of it.*

His dad then told him about Coach John Wooden, the legendary basketball coach at UCLA. Wooden once told his players, *"Your reputation is who other people think you are, but your character is the person you really are."*

Jason's dad went on to say, "The best way to be a person of high character is to make good choices in your life. Live your life in a way that you are proud of yourself. ***When you are honest and truthful, you never have to worry about the consequences of cheating or lying.***"

It was much easier to fall asleep. He felt that a huge weight had been lifted from his shoulders. He knew that tomorrow would be a better day.

Chapter 17

It's More Than A Game

Rocky Swenson saved the seat on the bus next to him for Jason. "Well, how did it go?" Rocky asked. Not waiting for a response he added, "Everyone has been asking about you."

Jason responded to Rocky's question with a question, "What did Coach Armstrong say?"

Rocky replied, "He didn't say too much, but he moved Perry Porter into your right guard spot. He said you were going to be late for practice. When you didn't show up he told Porter to be sure he knew his plays, because he may be starting at guard."

"What!" Jason responded, "he can't move me out of the starting lineup for just missing one practice. I had an excuse and Miss Kohler said she contacted him."

"What happened with Kohler anyway?" Rocky inquired.

Jason said, "It was all about a stupid vocabulary test. I got some answers from Brixton's paper and she found out."

"That's no big deal." Rocky added, "Kids do that all the time."

Jason elaborated, "I copied an entire page from his test."

"That's dumb," Rocky said. "You never should copy a whole page. No wonder you got caught."

Bringing the conversation back to football Jason asked, "What did you do at practice?"

Rocky explained that they mostly worked on offensive plays and the passing game. He told him that Perry Porter was making a lot of mistakes at right guard. "He jumped off sides a couple times, pulled the wrong way on the sweep, and really messed up the trap block. There is no way we can run the trap with him in there.

"You should have seen him on the 48 sweep. He pulled left and Markins pulled right like he was supposed to, and they smashed into each other right behind the center. It was a blast! Stackhouse told him it was the hardest hit he saw all year, but he hit his own man!"

Max pulled the bus up in front of school As Jason headed toward his locker he thought "Coach has got to put me back into the starting lineup."

The school day went well. Jason felt like his old self. Mrs. Kohler acted as if nothing happened and Brains seemed normal. "Maybe she didn't even talk with him," Jason thought.

His good news bubble burst when Coach Stackhouse approached him in the locker room. "Vershaw, step into my office for a minute."

Jason felt like he was heading for his execution. He didn't want to go, but was pulled by some unseen force that reminded him of his father's words, *"You have to accept personal responsibility for your actions and deal with the consequences."*

For a brief second he thought of his sixth grade teacher, Mrs. Gruber, and the mirror test. *"I should have followed her advice."*

The coaches' office was full of footballs, equipment, and play sheets. Coach Armstrong was already on the practice field to get the team organized. Coach Stackhouse motioned for Jason to sit in a chair next to his desk. As he sat down his right leg started trembling and he couldn't get it to stop. It seemed as if his entire body was shaking like he was out in freezing weather without a coat. Then he looked at his hands and they were wringing wet. He wondered if Coach could see how nervous he was.

Jason was looking at the floor when Coach Stackhouse said, "I want you to look at me, listen closely to what I have to say, and I want you to listen with your eyes and ears!"

Jason quickly made eye contact with Coach Stackhouse.

In a calm, clear voice Coach Stackhouse said, "I've spoken with Miss Kohler and your parents and they all agree with what I'm going to say."

Jason felt himself getting smaller and melting into his chair as Coach leaned forward and stared at him with his steel gray eyes.

Coach continued, "I'm not going to talk with you about the incident in Spanish class. Miss Kohler and your parents have discussed that with you. What I do want you to understand is that *football is more than a game. It is a commitment you make to the coaches and your teammates.* You made a bad decision and because of that you will not be starting in the opening game against Roselawn."

A tear trickled down Jason's cheek and he wiped his nose with his sleeve as he sniffed. He had his heart set on starting, his parents said they would be there, and he had a sense of satisfaction knowing how far he had come with his attitude about football. It wasn't very long ago when he was afraid of playing tackle football. Now he was looking forward to the game like a kid anticipating his birthday. His hopes and dreams were shattered!

Coach put his hand on Jason's shoulder and said, "Now listen closely. You can continue practicing with the team and you will dress for the game. Whether or not you play in the game, and how soon you get in, if you get in, depends on your attitude and behavior in practice. I expect you to be a real leader, hustle, and work hard to show the rest of the team that you deserve to play. *How you respond to my decision is up to you.* As far as I am concerned, you learned from your mistake and I'm going to look to the future."

To be certain they were thinking alike Coach Stackhouse asked Jason to repeat what he told him.

Jason related the coach's comments almost word for word.

"Great!" said Coach Stackhouse. "Now have one more thing for you to do. When we g out to practice all the players are going to b wondering what happened. I will call everyon together and explain the situation, and then I wan you to tell the team you are sorry about missin practice and that it won't happen again."

Jason thought, "Wow! That's going to b hard to do."

Coach interrupted his thinking and said "Will you do that?"

Jason really didn't know what to say. H thought for a few seconds, looked at Coach wiped the tears from his eyes and said, *"You ca count on me, Coach."*

"That a boy!" Coach replied. "Now go t the bathroom and blow your nose and we will jo out to the practice field together."

Coach Armstrong was just finishin stretching and conditioning drills when Coac Stackhouse and Jason arrived. Stackhouse blev his whistle and called for the boys to form a semi circle. He started out by saying, "Boys, we hav often said that *football is more than a game You are expected to do your best in school an on the field."* Then just like he said he would, h explained Jason's situation. He told the team tha Jason wanted to talk with them.

Jason's voice cracked at first, but it gaine strength as he went on. "…I made a bad decisio in Spanish class and had to miss practice yesterday. It won't happen again. I'm ready to work hard to prepare to beat Roselawn on Saturday."

Coach Stackhouse followed up with a few final words about the situation. "This incident is over. I don't want to hear any more about it. We will concentrate on getting ready to beat the Wolves. Let's welcome Jason back to the team with a big clap. One, two, three...!"

Chapter 18

Lead By Example

Wednesday's practice was devoted to special teams. Coach Stackhouse believed that the punting and kicking teams determined many games. Because of that, he spent more time than most middle school coaches working with the special teams.

The rules were adjusted at the seventh grade level to balance out the skills of the players. In the punting game, there was a three-second delay before the defense could rush the punter. Players catching punts could not advance the ball. That also eliminated tackling on punt returns.

Kickoff returns were the same as regular football, except the kicking team was allowed to kickoff from midfield and all long returns came back to the 50-yardline. That made it impossible for a real fast player to score with ease, but still provided the players with the opportunity to learn about pursuit angles and open field tackling. Bobby Benson and Jon Rynders, two of the fastest players on the team, were back deep to return kickoffs.

Coach Stackhouse liked to run a middle wedge return on kickoffs. The return man was instructed to catch the ball and take it up the middle behind a wedge of blockers. Coach Armstrong lined up a kickoff team to practice against the starting return team. Bobby caught the ball and broke up the middle behind his wedge of blockers. Just when he was going to break through a hole to the outside, a player broke through the wedge and made a jarring tackle.

The hit startled Benson. He usually had the opportunity to make a cut before being hit. He wondered who got down the field so fast and broke through the wedge. In addition to that, the tackler kept his feet and drove Bobby backward. That seldom happened.

Bobby looked over at who tackled him, and said, "Nice tackle, Jason." Coach Armstrong yelled encouragement, "That's the attitude, Jason."

The rest of the practice went much the same. Jason was the first one in line for drills and was impressive playing on the scout squad for special teams. He ran signal drill at the end of practice with the second team offense. Coach Stackhouse often would finish practice with what he called "Signal Drill." He divided the players into three offensive teams. Each group would run all the offensive plays down one side of the field and back up the other. The QB called the play, and then the players would sprint ten yards and jog twenty. Then the team would reset and run another play.

The coaches constantly checked alignment, snap count, and blocking responsibilities. The players went all out and were required to run as if they were going against a 5-2 defense. It was a great way to improve conditioning while still working on team skills. At times, the coaches would jump in on defense with a hand dummy to see if the correct player would block them.

Jason was a little frustrated running with the second team. He was used to lining up between Swenson and Brixton. They were starting to get used to each other. He noticed the first unit was delayed several times when Porter didn't know what to do, or when he did the wrong thing.

Coach Armstrong was always shouting encouragement. Jason could hear him all over the field. "Feet apart, stay low, carry out your fakes, step with the correct foot, carry the ball in the outside arm, fake like you run, run like you fake, anticipate the count, be quick!"

On the way back to the locker room, Coach Stackhouse jogged next to Jason and said, *"Nice job out there today. Keep it up!"*

Jason accepted the fact that he made a mistake and was determined to make a good impression on the coaches and the rest of the team. He wanted to play in the opening game and he decided to do what was required.

Coach Stackhouse told Jason that he would check with his teachers to make sure he was doing his best in the classroom. Coach believed in developing good habits. Several times in the first two weeks of practice he told the team, *"You make your habits and then your habits either make or break you."* At the team meeting after practice he wrote the following words on the chalkboard.

Behavior
▲
Attitudes
▲
Habits
▲
Actions
▲
Feelings
▲
Thoughts

He emphasized how important it is for a person to control their thinking since thoughts control feelings. Feelings control actions. Actions become habits. Habits influence attitudes, and attitudes determine behavior.

He asked the players, "Have you ever noticed someone with bad behavior? Sometimes people will blame a poor attitude for bad behavior, but really, the behavior is determined by the way the person is thinking. Most often it is the way they are thinking about themselves. If a person doesn't like himself or herself, it is difficult to like anyone else. That is another reason why you should live your life in a positive way. *Always remember the golden rule. Treat others the way you like to be treated.*"

Jason recalled similar comments from his parents. In fact, when he had a decision to make and he talked it over with his mother, she always helped him make a list and gather all the information critical to making the decision. Usually she ended by reminding him of the, *"mirror test."*

Jason finally saw the connection. Hmm, *"The way I treat others has a big influence on the way I feel about myself."* At that point, he decided to make a commitment to himself to always do his own work and to take the feelings of others into consideration when making decisions.

That night, on the way home on the bus, Jason sat with Rocky and they talked football. Only a couple practices remained and Rocky was

114

concerned because Perry Porter still didn't know all his plays. Perry was a decent student, but he seemed to panic during crucial situations in football. Unfortunately, every play was a crucial one.

Jason assured Rocky that he would get together with Perry tomorrow during lunch and make sure he knew his plays.

"Why should you help him?" Rocky asked. "He's playing your position. Maybe if you let him screw up, Coach will put you in the game."

"Look, Rocky," Jason pointed out, "***Perry is my teammate.*** He's an Eagle just like we are. I want him to play the best that he can. If I was in his place I would want someone to help me."

Rocky said, "I don't think I would do it."

Jason thought, "I remember when Coach told me that he expected me to be a 'leader' the rest of the week. I told him that I never considered myself a 'leader.' *He replied that everyone had to lead in some way and the most important person he had to lead was himself.*"

Coach Stackhouse told him, "Lead by example. Instead of just going along with the crowd when you see something wrong, *do the right thing because it is the right thing to do.*"

Jason's newly found wisdom was tested the following day when prior to school several of his friends found that the door to the lunchroom storage area had been left open. Tank suggested taking a couple boxes of potato chips - that no one would miss them.

Listening in on what the guys were planning to do, Jason went over to the door, opened it slightly, reached inside, turned the lock on the doorknob, and closed the door. Before anyone realized it, the door  was locked. Jason told the group, "We better head to class." The plot was stopped before it got started. Tank really didn't need the chips anyway.

Chapter 19

TINSTAAFL

Jason continued to lead the way in the classroom and on the field. He struggled in Spanish class, but Mrs. Kohler knew he was doing his own work. When she reminded the class: *"In the long run you are better off to do your own work and earn a 'B' or 'C' than you are to get answers from someone else and get an 'A.'"* Jason knew what she was talking about.

Science and math went reasonably well. He often volunteered in class and worked on projects with several different students. Ms. Marks, the science teacher, assigned students a variety of different partners for projects. She told the students that it was a good learning experience to team up with someone new rather than always going with their best friends.

Mr. Jensen knew how to keep the students interested in math class. He often combined math with social studies or some other class. To warm up the students he might do something like this:

"Think of the number of states in the United States (50). Add to that the number of the original colonies (13). Add to that total the number of Supreme Court Justices (9). Subtract from that the number of counties in Wisconsin (72). What is the answer (0)?"

He used facts that the students had learned in other classes and they had to do the math in their head.

The last couple practices were especially difficult for Jason. He was doing everything possible to show the coaches that he deserved to play. He even volunteered to return kickoffs against the varsity kickoff team. Whenever one of the coaches was giving instructions Jason made sure to listen with his eyes. He was the first one on the practice field and the last one off.

"I just know I will play in the game on Saturday," Jason thought as he picked up his game jersey after Friday's practice. Then he reviewed in his mind what Coach Stackhouse told him. "I've been doing my best in school and have been leading by example on the football field."

Since the jerseys were new this year Coach encouraged everyone to try them on to make sure they fit. Jason was hoping to get the same number his dad wore in high school, but since Jason was a lineman, coach told him he had to have a lineman's number. He was impressed with the bright red jersey and white numbers. The word "Eagles" was printed across the front of the jersey above the number.

"Gosh," Jason thought, "I'm number 64. My dad's number in high school was 32. I guess I will have to tell him that I'm going to be twice as good as he was."

Bobby Benson asked Coach Stackhouse if it was OK for him to get his name printed on the back of his jersey. Coach snapped back at him, "We are the 'Eagles' not the 'Bensons'." He reminded Bobby that he expected everyone to play as a team. *We don't have individual stars. We play together as a unit. It's not about personal attention; it's all about helping us be the best team that we can be.*

Coach Armstrong walked around the locker room making sure everyone had his jersey. He noticed quite a commotion around Tank's locker. Checking into the situation he found that Tank had his jersey on with the big number in

front. "Tank, the big number goes to the back,
Coach corrected him.

It was funny how all of the jerseys fi
differently. Tank could look down and read hi
number looking back up at him; only his 6
looked like 99 from his perspective. It wa
difficult to read Matt Mulroy's number. He wa
the smallest player on the team and with hi
jersey tucked in, his 8 almost looked like a C
Jason looked around the room and thought hov
proud he was to be a member of the Eagles team

Prior to sending everyone home for th
evening, Coach Stackhouse had a brief tean
meeting. He reminded the players to get a goo
night's sleep. He told the team that he expecte
everyone to be home and in bed by 9:00. He als
emphasized the value of being mentally prepare
to play their best game.

"Remember," Coach Stackhouse went on
"Concentrate on your play; don't worry about th
opponent. Roselawn usually has a big team an
they will try to intimidate you during warm-ups
but don't pay any attention to them. They wil
chant and shout more than we will, but tha
doesn't have any bearing on how good their tean
will be. *It is what you do __in__ the game tha
counts, not how much noise you make durin$
warm-ups.*"

Then Coach repeated something that h
said several times before. *"It's not the size of th*

dog in the fight that counts; it's the size of the fight in the dog. When we are ahead never let up, and if we are behind, never give up. Always do your best. We are looking for a 100% effort from everyone!"

Coach Stackhouse then walked over to the blackboard and wrote "TINSTAAFL." He asked the team, "Does anyone know what that means?" Not a hand went up. The team was silent. Coach said, "Always remember, 'TINSTAAFL'." He pointed to each letter as he explained the meaning. *"There – Is – No – Such – Thing – As – A – Free – Lunch."*

He went on to explain, *"If you want to get something in life you have to work for it. Just like in the classroom, if you want a good grade you have to apply yourself. Nothing comes without effort.* Keep that in mind during the game tomorrow. The coaches are looking for your best effort!"

Leaving the room to board the bus, Jason thought, "Hmm, 'TINSTAAFL,' there is no such thing as a free lunch."

Chapter 20

The Big Game

Jason was the first one up at the Vershaw house on Saturday morning. He sat at the desk in his room looking over the play list where he had carefully drawn in all of his responsibilities on every play. "I've got to know my plays," he told himself. *"The team is counting on me!"* After having reviewed all the blocking with Perry, Jason was more confident than ever.

Even though he didn't know if he would play, he was still anxious to get to school and prepare for the game. Coach Armstrong advised the players to eat just a light breakfast. To make his point he told the players, *"A hungry dog hunts best."*

As Jason was finishing his breakfast, his dad rubbed his head and asked, "Are you ready to go? We are looking forward to watching the game."

"You mean you are still coming to the game?" Jason asked.

Jason's mother replied, "Of course we wi be there."

"But I might not even play," Jasc reminded them.

Jason's dad said, "It is your first game c tackle football and we wouldn't miss it. Mak sure you are ready to play."

"Dad, I know all my plays and I've bee working hard at practice. I am ready to go. I ju hope Coach puts me in."

During the pre-game warm-ups, Jasc glanced over at the Roselawn squad and thoug! they looked much bigger than the Eagle Forgetting Coach Stackhouse's advice, all of sudden he began to doubt his ability to compe! against the Wolves. "Maybe it's OK that I'm no starting. Perhaps Coach will forget to put me i the game." He was determined not to sa anything to Coach Armstrong.

The game got off to a slow start for th Eagles. Their first play, a 31 Dive, was stuffe On the second play, a 48 Sweep, Porter pulled to flat and ran right into the wingback that wa blocking the defensive end. On the third play Moose Mullen's man ran right over him and h Levi as he was getting the handoff from Devil The ball rolled on the ground and a defender fe on it on the Eagle 32-yardline.

Three plays later the Wolves' outstanding quarterback connected on a 25-yard pass for a touchdown. The two-point conversion was stopped when Juan Gomez went up high to knock a pass down in the corner of the end zone. "That's the way to go up for the ball, Gomer!" Coach Armstrong yelled. It was about the only good thing that happened in the early stages of the game.

Benson returned the kickoff almost to midfield. On the first play Coach decided to have Komp throw a Pop Pass to Christian at left end. Devin took a one-step drop and fired the ball. "Smack!" The ball fell harmlessly to the ground. Coach Armstrong saw Moose on the grass and big number 77 strutting back to the defensive huddle. "That 77 is just eating us up out there!" Armstrong shouted at Stackhouse.

Coach Stackhouse called a timeout and as he entered the offensive huddle, he turned toward the bench and called out, "Vershaw!" Jason sat as if frozen to the bench. Coach Armstrong yelled, "Vershaw, get in there for Porter!"

Jason ran into the huddle yelling, "Porter! Porter!"

All eyes were on Coach Stackhouse as he calmly told the team, "Listen closely, here is what we are going to do. That 77 is really coming hard. We are going to fake the 29 Sweep, and run the 33 Trap. Remember now, Mullen, just let

77 penetrate and you block the linebacker. We need a good double team on the nose, and Vershaw you are trapping 77. Keep your head up and stay low; he won't be expecting it. Levi look for an outside cut, and Cole, get the block on the safety."

The referee warned Coach, "Ten seconds!" As he left the huddle Coach Stackhouse said, "Everyone do his job and we will take it all the way. Young, make sure you carry out a good fake."

Devin called the play, "Ok let's make it work, 33 Trap on Hit. Ready, block!" The players clapped their hands together and hustled up to the line of scrimmage.

Jason was concentrating on the count, "33 Trap on Hit." He ran the play often in practice and Coach told him to, ***"Drive through the defender, not just to the defender."*** He knew that Coach put the play in just for him because he was the quickest lineman on the team.

Number 77 for the Hawks was Tiger Dercks. He was at least 40 pounds heavier than Jason and the most aggressive player on the team. Tiger had never seen a trap block and when he was left unblocked, he rushed into the backfield to tackle the wingback, Josh Young, who was faking a sweep left. When he realized Young didn't have the ball, Dercks looked inside and saw a flash of bright red.

Jason's left shoulder pad made contact just above Tiger's left hip. He never knew what hit him. Jason kept his legs pumping and drove the big Wolves' lineman backward where he tripped over another player and made a pile. Jason felt a rush of excitement, but remembered Coach Armstrong's words, "When you get one block, go get another; be like a heat seeking missile."

Having gotten one block, he pushed off and headed downfield where he saw Levi cutting off Christian's block on the safety. As Jason sprinted to catch up he found himself running next to another Wolves player. He recalled Coach Armstrong's demonstration at practice, and how a defender 20 yards behind the runner really isn't a threat to make the tackle. Jason kep running past the player over to Levi, who was in the end zone handing the ball to the official.

"Way to go, Levi!" Jason patted him on the back. They were joined by more excited players, but they didn't overdo the celebration because on Friday's practice Coach Stackhous explained the rule that excessive demonstration are illegal and can result in a penalty.

He had instructed the team to always lin up for a two-point conversion unless he sent in the kicking team. The Eagles extra point tean still needed a lot of work so Coach planned to g for two points.

He decided to fake the 33 Trap that the just scored on, and run the Sweep Left. Sur enough, just like the coach planned, half of th Wolves team tackled Levi who took a good fak into the line, and Josh Young sprinted untouche into the end zone. Who made the key block o the linebacker? It was the pulling guard, Jaso Vershaw. The score read: Eagles 8 - Visitors 6.

"Wow!" Jason thought running off th field. "I never realized playing in the line coul be so much fun." As he headed back to the re: of the team on the sideline, he heard his mother' voice, "Way to go Eagles!" He glanced up in th stands and saw both his parents standing an clapping.

"I'm sure glad I didn't quit when things got tough," he said to himself.

Just then he heard a gruff, loud voice, "Let's focus on the game. We've got a lot of football left to play!"

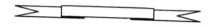

Success Section

Tips For Success From The Coaches

The Athlete's Alphabet

Regardless of what sport you play or what school activity you participate in, following *"The Athlete's Alphabet"* will help you be the best that you can be. These are the lessons in Jason's story.

Attitude – Your attitude is the way you mentally approach tasks every day. When you have a positive mental attitude (PMA), you believe you will be successful.

Belief – When you believe in yourself you have confidence that you will succeed. Belief comes from positive practice and preparation. Always practice to get better - not to get it over.

Courage – It takes courage to overcome fear. Fear of making a mistake makes it difficult to do your best. When you have courage you do the right thing because it is the right thing to do.

Desire – In order to be successful at any task, it takes Deep Down Desire (DDD) to take on the challenge and do your best. When you possess desire you have the drive to be successful.

Enthusiasm - You perform at your highest level when you are excited about what you are doing. Desire coupled with enthusiasm helps a person succeed. This is referred to as, "The fire of desire." To be "fired up" means you are excited about a sport.

Failure – Failure is a temporary setback or the inability to complete a task. Failure is a great learning experience. It is like fertilizer; it helps us grow. Glance at failure and learn from it, but stay focused on success.

Goals – When you expect to accomplish a specific task you establish the goal of attaining it. Goals give us direction in games and in life. Your goal in practice is to improve, not to just get it over. Always practice and play with a purpose or goal.

Hustle – You are hustling when you practice and play in an alert, aggressive manner. Coaches notice players who put out a great effort. Everyone has the ability to hustle and play with enthusiasm.

Integrity – When you are truthful and honest you have integrity. Others trust you when you build a reputation for being honest. The best teams are made up of players who trust each other.

Jealousy – Doing your best is more important than being the best. Jealous people resent the achievements of others and often hope that others fail. This type of thinking gets in the way of your ability to succeed. Focus on your performance.

Knowledge – Study and learn as much as possible about your activity. When you know the rules and understand the fundamentals of your sport, you are prepared to be successful. Knowledge is power!

Loyalty – A good team player is faithful or loyal to the team by following the rules and working hard at all practices. When you are loyal, you make a commitment to your teammates and coaches to do your best.

Motivation – Motivation refers to your reason to take action. When you are motivated you have the desire to do your best. There are three types of motivation: fear, reward, and attitude. Attitude is the best because it is personal and you control it.

Negative Attitude – When you begin sentences with, "If'a, would'a, could'a, should'a, yeah but, and maybe," you are being negative. "I can't" and "why me" are also negative and must be eliminated. Replace these with "I can" and "I will."

Opportunity – You have a great opportunity when the potential for achievement exists. All challenges present opportunities for success. When you have a positive attitude, instead of obstacles you see opportunities.

Persistence – Persistence is a state of mind where you continue to do your best in spite of setbacks. When you are persistent you never give up or quit. In a game, forget about mistakes, and look forward to the next play.

Quit – Quitting is the act of giving up or failing to do your best. It is a selfish act because it is done without concern for the welfare of the team. Quitting can be habit forming and must be avoided. If you decide a sport is not for you, speak with your coach.

Respect – By treating others with respect you hold them in high regard and consider their welfare before you act. It is important to show respect for yourself and others.

Sportsmanship – Sportsmanship is the conduct of one playing a sport. This includes: fairness, respect for your teammates, coaches, officials, opponents, and yourself, and graciousness in winning or losing.

Teamwork – Teamwork is the ability to cooperate with others to act in a manner that places the value of the team above that of any individual. Teamwork is essential in order for any group to perform to its full potential.

Unity – A team has great unity when team members realize what is best for the team is more important than individual recognition. Coaches often refer to this as, "Playing together as a unit." Good team members aren't concerned about statistics and individual recognition.

Victory – Coaches, players, parents, and fans all value being victorious. It is important to remember that every player is a winner when he or she makes a commitment to the team and does his or her best in practice and games.

Work – It is essential for all athletes to develop a winning work ethic. This means you do your best even when no one is watching. Work hard, but also work smart. Always practice hard to get better. Players who work hard always hustle.

X - In Algebra "X" is the unknown quantity. In sports you are "X." No one really knows how good you can become. Your commitment to practice and willingness to listen to your coaches and work hard will determine how much you improve.

You - You are the key to your future success. No one can instill in you the drive to achieve. Coaches, teammates, friends, fans, and parents can inspire you, but true desire to play your best must come from within. The "mirror test" is best judge of your character and effort.

Zone – Top athletes play the best when they are "in the zone." This means they don't worry about what might go wrong or think about every move, but have fun playing the game. "Getting in the zone" comes as a result of dedicated practice and always working to improve.

Sportsmanship Checklist

Play every game in the spirit of good sportsmanship. Coach Stackhouse gave his players this checklist to make sure his players were good sports. How do you shape up?

_____ 1. **Play By The Rules** – I follow all the rules.

_____ 2. **Respect The Officials** – I concentrate on my play and always respect the officials.

_____ 3. **Communicate In A Positive Manner** – I am positive when communicating with teammates and coaches.

_____ 4. **Practice Self-Control** – I keep my emotions under control and focus on my performance.

_____ 5. **Be A Positive Example** – I set an excellent example for others to follow.

_____ 6. **Make Positive Comments** – I stay away from trash talk and never taunt opponents.

_____ 7. **Admit Your Mistakes** – I take personal responsibility for my play and never make excuses.

_____ 8. **Be A Team Player** – I value the success of the team ahead of individual praise and recognition.

_____ 9. **Always Give 100%** - I play with pride and do my best at all times.

_____ 10. **Credit The Opponent** – Win or lose I give credit to the opponent after a tough game.

_____ 11. **Play With Class** – I concentrate on playing the game and never show off.

_____ 12. **Be Honest** - I take pride in being honest and in keeping my word.

_____ 13. **Follow All Training Rules** – I make good decisions and follow all team rules.

_____ 14. **Have Fun** – I enjoy the spirit of competition and enjoy being with my teammates.

The Coaches' Favorite Sayings

1. Good, better, best, never let it rest, until your good get better, and your better gets best!
2. Attitudes are contagious; make sure yours is worth catching.
3. Instead of barriers see hurdles.
4. Instead of obstacles see opportunities.
5. Instead of problems see solutions.
6. Keep your eyes on the prize.
7. Doing your best is more important than being the best.
8. Listen with your eyes.
9. Do the right thing because it is the right thing to do.
10. There is no "I" in Team.
11. T.E.A.M. Together Everyone Achieves More.
12. All the way with PMA! Positive Mental Attitude.
13. Pound ground to gain ground.
14. An inch is a cinch; but a yard is hard.
15. The body can only achieve what the mind can perceive.
16. Do the little things right and the big things happen.
17. Practice to get better - not to get it over.
18. P. P. & P - Positive Practice and Preparation.

19. D. D. D. - Deep Down Desire.

20. Don't say you will try; tell me you will do your best.

21. Do it because it's hard.

22. It takes a lifetime to build a reputation; one incident to destroy it.

23. Respect everyone, but fear no one.

24. Focus on what you can control.

25. Play hard, but also play smart.

26. Better than yesterday, not as good as tomorrow.

27. Play with pride!

28. Courage is overcoming fear.

29. Commitment means you can count on me.

30. The most important play is the one coming up.

31. TINSTAAFL – There Is No Such Thing As A Free Lunch.

32. A hungry dog hunts best.

33. You make your habits; your habits make or break you.

34. The team is counting on you.

35. It's not the size of the dog in the fight that counts; it's the size of the fight in the dog.

The Book and the Author

To order additional copies of *It's More Than A Game!* contact Bill Collar at (<u>pma@billcollar.com</u>) or by phone (920) 833-6064. Visit Bill's Web site a (<u>www.billcollar.com</u>). Teacher's guides are available Special pricing consideration is granted for orders of a dozen or more.

Bill has also written: ***Exceeding the Standards Teaching with Pride, Poise, and Passion.*** The book assists the reader in paving the path to personal and professional peak performance through sharing hints and tips from Bill's career. The book is recommended for al educators and adults who are striving for excellence i their field.

Bill Collar taught high school and coached for 3: years. He was recognized as WI State Teacher of the Year, WI Coach of the Year and coached state champion in football and track. An innovative teacher, Bill taugh history in reverse chronological order and integrated U.S History with American Literature. He also designed Native American History class and co-taught a uniqu Great Issues class. Now a professional speaker, Bill ha addressed over 500 audiences in his career. He i available for workshops and staff development.